W9-AGV-069

# OUT OF NOWHERE

*A Selection of Titles by Susan Dunlap*

*The Darcy Lott Series*

A SINGLE EYE
HUNGRY GHOSTS
CIVIL TWILIGHT
POWER SLIDE
NO FOOTPRINTS
SWITCHBACK *
OUT OF NOWHERE *

* *available from Severn House*


## ACKNOWLEDGMENTS

I am grateful to writers Linda Grant and Gillian Roberts for their careful reading and good suggestions at the time when giving them is the hardest.

Thanks once again to stuntwoman/stunt coordinator Carolyn Day for her willingness to share her expertise.

As always, many thanks to my superb literary agent, Dominick Abel.

# OUT OF NOWHERE

Susan Dunlap

This first world edition published 2016
in Great Britain and the USA by
SEVERN HOUSE PUBLISHERS LTD of
19 Cedar Road, Sutton, Surrey, England, SM2 5DA.
Trade paperback edition first published
in Great Britain and the USA 2016 by
SEVERN HOUSE PUBLISHERS LTD



British Library Cataloguing in Publication Data
A CIP catalogue record for this title is available from the British Library.

ISBN-13: 978-0-7278-8601-9 (cased)
ISBN-13: 978-1-84751-723-4 (trade paper)
ISBN-13: 978-1-78010-784-4 (e-book)

*To Emily Lambert, with love.*



*All Severn House titles are printed on acid-free paper.*

Severn House Publishers support the Forest Stewardship Council™ [FSC™],
the leading international forest certification organisation.
All our titles that are printed on FSC certified paper carry the FSC logo.

Typeset by Palimpsest Book Production Ltd.,
Falkirk, Stirlingshire, Scotland.
Printed and bound in Great Britain by
TJ International, Padstow, Cornwall.

# ONE

Another time I might have wondered why my favorite brother was so keen to meet me halfway out on Pier 39. But when I got his text I was just glad to blow off energy with the run. And eager, as always, to see him.

I whipped out of my room in the Zen Center, ignoring the ominous sky, and took off.

The first shower spit down on me ten minutes later. I could have gone back for a slicker.

I hate going back.

A minute later it was raining. I could have slowed down and watched my step.

I hate slowing down.

Most of all I hate waiting. My last movie gig didn't end well. A stunt double/stunt coordinator linked to disaster is what Hollywood superstitions are made of. I'd be waiting a while for the next call.

*Get over yourself!* Zen teachings might say. What they do say is, *Do the next thing.* So I'd been taking stretch classes, weight classes, practicing tightrope and slack wire walking, teaching my brother, Mike, camera work, and being surprised at what he had picked up in his two decades away. We'd shot a couple of wire-work promos that I'll send out after enough time has passed. It was like when we were teenagers, me doing the stunts, him manning the camera and keeping an eye out for cops or family, whoever's rules we might be trespassing. We never got caught.

By the time I hit the slippery boards of Pier 39, San Francisco's big tourist attraction, tourists were flooding toward the street. The rain had washed away the pier's jugglers, acrobats and magicians. Shopkeepers were huddling behind closed doors or pulling down grates. The pier was nearly empty. I was soaked and shivering and hoping to spot Mike in the doorway of a nice warm bar.

Even so, I almost missed my brother.

'Omigod, Mike. You look awful.'

Another time he would have snarked, 'Thanks.' Now he didn't expend the effort. He looked like just thinking was a strain, like balancing on his two feet was hard. My brother, who hated slowing down as much as I did, who never considered going back.

'What happened to you?'

A gust slammed into the pier. Bay water shot across the wooden walk. A garbage can tottered, crashed down on its side, and rolled. An ill-anchored sunglasses cart had broken loose, flinging colored plastic like confetti. It had nearly hit me as I'd run toward this miserable spot Mike had chosen. The wind was yanking my hair from the rubber band and snapping red strands in my face. His hair, shorter, swirled like maple leaves on a tree.

I tried to think how long it had been since I'd seen him. Two weeks? Three? My tall, buff brother who never missed a morning run? How could he have crumbled to this? I reached a palm toward his forehead. 'Are you sick?'

He almost smiled. 'If I was sick, I wouldn't have called *you.*'

True enough. We've got a sister who's a doctor. I let my hand drop to his shoulder. 'But you did. So? What's going on with you? Tell me. Trust me.'

*I do trust* . . . hung on his lips. But he caught himself. I gave him points for that. I was asking a lot. He'd spent twenty years looking over his shoulder.

'I don't . . . I'd tell you if I could. I'm not scamming you. I don't know why this is happening.'

'Why *what* is happening?'

He was not a fidgeter; he'd trained himself free of quirks and tics, to give no early warning. So, it didn't surprise me that he stood utterly still a moment before answering me. 'First, I got sideswiped crossing Columbus after work last week.'

'A car hit you? Were you hurt?'

'Hard on my jacket, but I was OK. Too dark to see the car. I figured bad driver.'

I nodded. What anyone would think. What a number of pedestrians in this city should have thought sooner.

'Same thing outside my place. Four days later. Before dawn. Going for my morning run. Car slammed into me in the crosswalk. Threw me against a trash can.'

'Omigod! Were you—'

'Injured? Not much. Bruises. Too dark to see more of the car than old, dark, probably four door.' He conjured up a watery smile. 'Figured bad driver. Good driver would have aimed better.'

I grabbed his arms. We were both shaking. 'Why?'

'I don't know!'

'What have you done? I mean, to find out?'

'Hit-and-run in the dark? No witnesses. It's a dead end.'

'Mike! You lived in the shadows for twenty years; this can't be the first time you were targeted for something. What did you do then?'

He stared at me like I'd missed the obvious. 'I left.'

*Of course.*

'I had no ties. If things got bad, I moved on. Better for everyone. But . . . I can't, not now.'

I nodded. He'd been home less than a year after being missing all that time. He couldn't leave again. Couldn't do that to the rest of us in the family.

I was the one who'd tracked him down, brought him home.

Rain slashed our shoulders, our heads. Pier 39 was dead empty now. My brother and I stood shifting like boxers in the erratic protection of the shop fronts. Kiosk shutters rattled. Mike pulled me in farther under the overhang of a deserted sushi place, blocking the storm with his body. Like he had the time he took me on my first walk up Haight Street when I was ten and he fourteen. It was quieter here under the overhang, but we were no less exposed to view and he shot glances in both directions before speaking.

'This is my problem, I need to—'

'If it's so dangerous, tell John.'

'Yeah, right.'

Which meant that Mike was into something he didn't want to reveal to our older brother, the former cop. Didn't want John to be conflicted. Or humiliated in front of his cop friends. Or feel he had to turn in his own brother. Or become an accessory.

'Gary then,' I shouted, the wind covering my panic. 'Hire him. Attorney–client privilege. He grew up keeping secrets from John.'

'Can't. Look, if I knew where this would lead, I'd know what to do. If I tell them, they'll be all over the place, probably making things worse. I hate involving even you. Especially you. If anything happened—'

'It won't. I can take care of myself.' *Better than you, apparently*, but I didn't say that.

'I can handle this. Trust me.'

Another time I would have nudged him and we'd have laughed at how much alike we sounded. Not surprising: we were the youngest of seven, him my protector since my first step. Now, I realized, things had flipped.

*You can handle this? So, why'd you call me?* But I knew the answer. If I was frantic and all roads were dead ends, I'd have called him. 'How long since you've slept?'

'More than an hour? Couple days?'

'Eaten?'

He shrugged. I'd never seen him stumped before. He looked like his innards had been sucked out of him

A seagull landed on the pier. Mike was gazing at it as if it held the answer. It did: *Sitting duck.*

'You were almost killed—'

He started to protest but caught himself. I gave him points for realizing the danger. For not making me put his precarious situation into words.

'OK,' I said, 'here's the plan. Don't even go back to your apartment. Take them . . .' I pulled out all the bills in my wallet and thrust them toward him. 'Don't argue. Get on the ferry to Larkspur—'

'I—'

'Give yourself a week to sleep, think straight, start playing offense.'

'A week!'

'OK, a couple days. You bounce back quick.'

'I can handle—'

'Get on the ferry. Disappear! That's what you're good at!' It was a low blow. He'd taken the ferry when he'd vanished before. 'Get a throwaway phone. Leave me a number on the zendo landline. Call my cell if you have to. OK?'

He just stood, jacket shimmying in the wind.

'Answer me this. I'm guessing not everything you did in the time you were gone was legal.'

'Yeah, but feds don't sideswipe you in the street.'

'Not often, anyway.' I nodded. 'Who else would come after you?'

'Geez, Darce, don't you think I've asked myself that? At first I thought it could be connected with my building. They're renovating the apartments, trying to harass tenants into leaving.' He looked around, as if the doors of the closed shops might be eavesdropping. 'Someone might have been trying to get in my apartment. I had the feeling, you know? But nothing was gone. No signs. Neighbors didn't see anything. Maybe I was imagining it.'

'Why would—'

'No idea.'

'What did you—'

'I got a house-sit in the Haight for a week.'

'And?'

'I just moved my stuff. But unless I hide in the closet, that's not going to make any difference. I'm not exactly invisible.'

I smiled. My tall, red-headed brother. Women eyed him in the street. When we walked together, people actually stopped and stared. 'Ex-lover, maybe?'

'It's been a slow winter.'

'Ex-friends? Business associates? Maybe you offended a gang member? Or you saw something you shouldn't have?'

'I called friends and not-so-friends, checked places I used to work. If I didn't have their numbers, I drove by. No one's targeting Gary's law office, or Hugo's Stop and Nosh, or Jansen's Burritos. Remember them?'

'Gang? Something you saw or heard?'

'Jeez, Darce, don't you think I've considered all that? I'm just living my life, going to State, trying to get myself grounded in normality. You couldn't be more boring and normal than me.'

'Dig deeper.'

'I dug. Really. Back off! If it was someone I shorted, or lied to about who I was, they'd write, they'd call, they'd threaten. There's been none of that. No way for me to make it right, whatever "it" is. It's like someone's kidnapped me and left no ransom note.'

Maybe he was right. Maybe he was too wasted to think deeply

enough. He was working at capacity answering my questions. And yet I could see the slight easing in his shoulders, his jaw just a bit less tense now that it wasn't just him alone in this.

I pulled him close, him the last person I ever wanted to disappear again, kissed his chin like I did when that was all I could reach. 'Go!'

He hesitated, my always-on-top-of-things brother. He leaned in as if about to hug me hard, caught himself, glanced both ways along the pier.

That frightened me more than anything he'd said.

He reached in his pants pocket, handed me his keys, turned and was gone.

It was all I could do not to run after him, to drag him back, to go with him on that ferry across the bay. For a wretched instant I knew for certain I would never see him again.

But, of course, I would. I am the number one believer in Mike. But I am also his sister and childhood co-conspirator. So, I pulled out a black watch cap to cover my own red hair and I tailed him, half-running through the dusky rain, feet smacking on the empty wooden walkway of the pier. I eyed each closed shop, each passageway between them to the back of the pier, every one of the many, shadowy spots to wait and watch. Nothing moved, which meant nothing. If someone had followed him, time was on their side. Mike was moving fast, but not too quickly for anyone to catch him.

The pier widened into a plaza and ended at Bay Street. I looked right.

Nothing moved.

I blurred my vision so only movement showed.

There he was. By the ferry ticket kiosk. Just like he said!

A naïve person would have smiled and left. Not I. I stepped into a doorway and watched my brother walk across the cement to the ramp, as casually as if the wind was not blowing rain sideways against him, and onto the waiting ferry.

On board, he turned, let his eyes roam the city view like a tourist might. He paused almost infinitesimally when he spotted me, as he knew he would.

A person who hadn't leapt from boat to dock in a stunt that ended up getting cut in post-production might have left then.

I waited till the ferry chugged out into the bay, till it almost disappeared behind the veil of rain and was halfway across the bay to Larkspur.

If he had managed to get back to the dock, I would have been furious, but not surprised. Even wiped out as he was.

My brother had handed me the keys but he hadn't told me where he'd left the car. That said something about his state of mind.

Mine, too.

# TWO

It took me a full half-hour slogging up and down dusky streets to spot the old Honda Civic. The rain had stopped as if, its day's work completed, it had clocked out. But the wind still held water. My running shoes squeaked on the wet sidewalks, sloshed in the crosswalks. I had the feeling someone was following me, but the couple times I snapped around to catch him, all I saw was blur, like there was a clear shower curtain hung around me.

When I spotted the car, on Bay Street near Embarcadero, I didn't even pause to check it out, but kept on around the corner, waited and peered back, hoping for a clear shot of the guy. In vain.

Chances were I'd been listening to my 'avoid-danger' spiel more than Mike had. Still I circled the block, before sliding down onto the driver's seat, wrapping myself in a huge old brown towel Mike had abandoned on the passenger side floor and checking the mirrors, the rearview, the driver's side (the Honda came off the line before anyone thought of the passenger side), one nearly hanging off the ceiling above the rearview and, I discovered, two small round jobs glued up above the corners of the windshield. Mike's additions. Glued in place since I was in here a month ago. The array let the driver see the blind spots, behind both side doors, and by the rear bumper – where an assailant would be poised to attack. Mike had been pulling out all stops.

And he'd failed.

My brother, who had always been able to handle anything . . .

But, dammit, I would not fail.

I made the rounds, checking each mirror, silently daring the assailant. 'You think I'm a sitting duck here? Bring it on!'

Zen and other meditation practices emphasize bare awareness. Notice the sounds, the feelings, the sights, all without stopping to name and categorize them. It's a hard practice to hear the fog horn without thinking 'fog horn' and easing into thoughts about fog horns I have known. Like when the 49ers score. Like . . . Just listening, just looking is hard. But here, now, it was perfect. Without moving my head I scanned the mirrors, from rain-blur to rain-blur, alert for movement, listened to cars starting and stopping, wind gust flapping an awning, for footfalls. 'Bring it!'

I was almost dry, sitting on a padded seat. I could wait him out. I shifted my glance from mirror to mirror, squinting against the increasing darkness. I let my gaze become specific now, noting cars, watching for repeat circlers.

What I noticed was the sign ahead, almost out of view: *Loading Zone*.

I laughed.

The Honda had to have been sitting here, in this primo tourist district for at least an hour. Any other car would have tickets lined up under the window wipers.

I started it up and slid into traffic.

A meter maid came around the corner.

I saluted and kept moving.

Three hours later, having showered, eaten and sat zazen in the zendo, I pushed open the passenger door for my Zen teacher, Leo Garson. Formally, Garson-roshi. It was just 7.00 p.m. The rain was gone, the street so dry I could have imagined the storm. Leo was headed for a priests' meeting at Zen Center San Francisco near the other end of Haight Street from Mike's block. 'And you?' he asked as I pulled into the sparse twilight traffic.

'Going to eyeball Mike's place.'

'Isn't that in Noe Valley?' i.e. not in the direction I was headed.

'His building's being renovated. He's got a house-sit near the Park.'

Anyone else would have sneered, 'Renovated! Prelude to being evicted.' But Leo makes a point of focusing on things as they are, not assuming what they soon will be. 'Don't assume,' he tells me more often than he should have to.

'This is just between us,' I said.

He grinned. He sees students week after week for private discussions of their Zen practice. 'Just between us' is his life.

I summarized the events on the pier. 'Mike has no idea why he's being targeted. These attacks are escalating. There may not be anything useful in his apartment, especially since he's just there for a few days, but someone may have been trying to get into the place he left. With luck I'll spot what they were after. I don't know where else to start.'

I expected Leo to tell me to be aware or careful, not to assume. What he said was, 'What do you know?'

'Maybe—'

'Start with what you *know*.'

'Things as they are?' I said, quoting the Zen dictum.

'Right. Even if you've told me before.'

'OK. Mike's been back in town less than a year. Before that he was missing for twenty years. Before that he was nineteen years old. Surely this can't be connected to him as a teenager.'

'Don't assume.'

I turned onto Broadway, headed west past topless clubs and Thai restaurants, crossed Columbus Avenue and Broadway suddenly became Chinatown. In two blocks we'd be in the tunnel. When we came out we'd cross Polk Street, the original gay mecca. 'Admittedly he dabbled on the far side of the law. He was working with a dirty cop. But the cop managed to go on living all those years Mike was missing, so how dangerous could that have been? And Mike was just a kid. Nothing that long ago would merit this level of attack.'

Leo didn't say I'd piled assumption on assumption.

Before he could reconsider I said, 'So then, after the Loma Prieta earthquake he disappeared. At first we assumed he was just in some other part of the city, helping to dig out rubble or feed the people whose homes had crumbled. Everyone in my family was doing what they could. John and all the other cops were doing double shifts, Gracie was at the hospital, Gary was somewhere. The phones were down. No one knew where anyone was. So, it was a couple weeks before we really began to worry about Mike.'

'And this year you found him and brought him back home.'

*Home to this! To be threatened!* We'd all been searching in our own ways, but I was the one who had put things together to find him. I was the one who'd pulled him out of his safe life in hiding and exposed him to this! I cut right, too fast, nearly clipped a Subaru.

Leo didn't comment; didn't even grab the door bar or brace his feet.

'What do I actually know about him during the years he was gone?'

Leo nodded.

'He was involved in tree-sitting to protect the redwoods from becoming deck furniture, but the lumber companies wouldn't be biding their time waiting to hit him. He cooked at a bare bones spa in the Mexican mountains. Drugs? Minor drugs, probably. But nothing worth assault.

'OK,' I had to admit, 'what I know is just about nothing.'

'And now?'

'He's been doing some legal research-ish work for Gary, so that's legal – and if he did come across anything incriminating, he'd have told Gary. Threatening Mike would only bring the problem front and center to Gary.'

'Friends? Lovers? Hobbies?'

'You sound like a questionnaire.' I turned on to Gough and started downhill. Gough is four lanes of vehicles headed with purpose, switching lanes while focused on beating the timed lights lest they be condemned to listen to their engines idle as drivers on the cross streets sail by. Leo sat silent while I cut across the four lanes and hung a right on Page. 'True answer? I don't know. Mike is the master of telling you nothing without you realizing it. If this threat hadn't come up, I wouldn't even have known he moved. He could—'

'You speculate.'

'Leo! Speculation is all I've got.'

'Speculation is what you think you've got.' When I didn't answer, he added, 'Just be clear what you're doing.'

'Don't assume?'

Now he smiled. 'Right.' With that, he pushed open the door, hesitated, and stayed in his seat. 'Darcy, you are very worried, more so than even the hit-and-runs merit. Why is that? What do you know that makes you frightened?'

I sat, listening to the engine balance against the brakes, feeling the little car being shaken by the wind, shivering in the draft from Leo's open door. What did I know? 'I get Mike.' The words seemed to burst out on their own. 'I adore him.'

Leo smiled.

'But I'm not blind to him. He's clever, resourceful, and

charming. He can do anything he puts his mind to. It never occurs to him that he might fail. So, he never has a plan B.'

The wind through the open door rustled my hair against my neck. 'Because,' I said, speaking as if reading off a teleprompter, as if I was seeing the words for the first time, 'he has no Plan B, he hasn't thought about the consequences of his first plan failing. He leaps for a ledge without a thought as to how far down the ground is.'

'And who might be standing underneath?' Leo said.

It sounded so damning that I could barely make myself nod yes. And when he stepped out and shut the door, the sudden stillness seemed not warmer but ominous.

I pulled into traffic, cut left and then right on to Haight Street, and headed toward Golden Gate Park. Each block became shabbier than the previous one, as if it were a trip back in time, decade by decade, block by block. Somewhere in the middle was the era when Mike had taken ten-year-old me on my first walk up the Summer of Love turned needle-culture street. Me wide-eyed as we stopped in head shops and vintage clothes stores. He'd bought me a peacock feather I still had in my room when he disappeared five years later.

It didn't surprise me that his address now was off the far end, near the park, between Haight and Golden Gate Park panhandle, which forms the northern edge of the Haight Ashbury district. Some of the buildings on Mike's street had been repaired and repainted. A Victorian next to the corner now had two-color window trim to spice up its respectable beige paint. Only one small gang tag marred the garage door. But Mike's building – two units up a staircase next to the garage – had withstood gentrification. A board covered one of the garage windows. Paint had been trod off the outside stairs. The place might have had a rental sign: *Not much for not much.*

All the parking spots were filled and I ended up circling around three times, giving up, and finally finding a place half a mile away on the far side of Kezar Stadium in Golden Gate Park. The Honda was a good-luck car. In all the time it had waited for Mike's return it had never been scratched, towed, ticketed, or stolen. But luck can do only so much.

So I loped back along the dark roadway, past cars speeding

out of the park toward the panhandle and downtown. The run was good. The sky had cleared and it was a standard cool April night. Now, on Mike's block, the air smelled vaguely of mud from the panhandle, of garlic and tomato from Haight Street, of pot. I eyed the buildings across the street, looking for a shadowy spot from which to check out Mike's building. There's a lot more social leeway on a block like this than in other neighborhoods. I found a dry spot on the bottom step of a six-plex, leaned back and observed.

You can observe for hours. There are tales of private eyes in danger of mummification. Maybe it was them balancing me to create the law of averages, but I sat for no more than twenty minutes.

The bay window of Mike's apartment was dark, but not curtained. As if he'd been taunting his attacker. I could make out the back of a sofa. A mirror or maybe a wide doorway behind it.

And something moving.

I shifted closer. Something low, like a guy squat-walking.

Had I imagined . . .?

No, there he – she? – was, a brush of hair showing over the line of the couch. Darker against dark in the black-and-white frame of the street light. Rising with each step. It's hard to squat-walk for long.

And gone. Out of frame of the window. I strained to see more clearly. Uselessly. Gone is gone.

But he was still in there. Only that one set of windows faced the street.

Odds were against it, but the intruder could be innocent. A friend from one of Mike's other incarnations.

I could wait and . . .

I couldn't.

# THREE

Keys in hand, I raced up the five steps and into the foyer of Mike's building, a dark space just large enough for the staircase and the doors. A sliver of light from the street eased through a high slit window. The ceiling fixture bulb was gone. Landlords do not remove bulbs and neglect to replace them. Bulbs don't unscrew themselves.

I half-expected the apartment door to fly open and the invader to come flying at me. And the upstairs neighbor to come stomping down, complaining about the noise.

What do you *know?*

I stood, feeling my breath moving in and out, suddenly aware how loud it was.

I made myself wait. Other sounds filled the void, the thrum of music system upstairs, the rise and fall of passing cars, a dog barking furiously then not at all. A crackle. From Mike's apartment, nothing.

Ear to the door, I strained.

Nothing.

I could wait. Anyone inside had to pass me on the way out. I'd hear him nearing the door. I could wait.

Waiting is not my strong suit.

I stuck the key in the lock, turned, flung the door open and jumped out of the line of fire.

Nothing! No shot, no gunman, no one racing out, no footfalls. Zip. Not even a curious neighbor.

I shoved the door against the wall. No one behind it. Scanning the room, I took a step inside.

Then I smelled it. 'Gas!'

The place reeked.

I raced upstairs, taking the steps two at a time, and banged on the neighbor's door. 'Gas! Get out! Gas!'

An old guy in old jeans and white T-shirt stumbled to the door. 'Huh?'

'Gas leak downstairs! Get out quick!' I checked him again. Half-asleep? Stoned? Or just out of it? 'You need to go now!'

He didn't move. I grabbed for his arm.

'Hey, I'm not dead yet!'

'Hurry!' I ran back down and waited in the shadows by Mike's door to see how 'not dead' the neighbor really was. He was moving fast when he passed me. I should have followed him out onto the street. Across the street. But Mike's apartment was my only hope of a lead. If it blew it could destroy the only chance of saving Mike. I had time for a glance at least. Surely.

Holding my breath, I rushed in, ran to the bay of windows, shoving the end of the sofa out of the way. The middle was a stationary pane. The whole affair was wooden and old. I braced my hands on the window near the kitchen and pushed up.

Painted stuck.

The gas was getting stronger by the moment. I needed to get out of here. Fighting not to inhale, I bent low, shoved like I was lifting a car off a baby. The window didn't move. I gave it one last push. It held. Then the paint cracked and the window creaked up. Gratefully I stuck my head outside and gasped for breath.

Which was why I heard the crash.

I just about fell over Mike's upstairs neighbor at the bottom of the stairs, standing alone on the sidewalk, holding a huge wrench.

'Did you turn off the gas?'

His eyes shot to the wrench and back to me.

'Did you see the crash?'

He shrugged.

On the far side of the street, safely, a clutch of people looked and murmured.

'Hey! The gas was on! The apartment was full of it. Just now there was a crash right outside, here! Big crash. Like someone threw a Volvo out the window. A minute ago!'

'Oh that.' He nodded. His head was big for his small, unhealthily thin body; his face was dark, lined, like a chestnut left out over the winter. He coughed, one of those coughs that seemed as much a part of him as his loose white T-shirt and his saggy jeans.

'What do you mean, *Oh that*?'

'Garbage. Some asshole throwing their cans and bottles in the can. Most cans are plastic. Not mine! I called the garbage crooks; I'm entitled to a decent can, but they say this one's fine. Fine? Right. Can's metal. Beer cans are aluminum, bottles are glass, crashing into the metal can, banging around everything in it. If I hear that once a day I hear it five times. Ten times. People got no consideration.'

I was staring. I muttered, 'Gas!' swallowed, and added, 'The whole building could have blown up. Someone turned on the gas. You could be dead!' *Mike* could be dead!

The man looked unimpressed.

The hell to him. 'Are the garbage cans under a window?'

'Yeah, haven't you been listening? People don't listen anymore. Yeah, right under the damned window. That's how come they can throw their cans and bottles in. If you lived here—'

But I was already halfway around the front of the building. The trash alley was a tunnel to the backyard, level with the garage. Above that passageway the adjacent buildings touched. Right in front of it, directly below an open side window in Mike's apartment, wedged now between buildings, was the dented metal trash can. Not exactly a catcher bag like we use to cushion high fall gags in the stunt world. The jumper could have hit the garbage can at an angle and careened off on to his neck. Or crashed through the lid and be stuck there like a candle in sand. Or come face to face with a neighbor taking out the garbage.

He'd been very lucky.

Which meant I would not be. No likely witnesses, no easy lead to him.

I squeezed by the can and made my way down the passage. It opened onto a small, ivy-carpeted yard, half-covered by stairs to the flat above. Oddly, the yard was not fenced, a rarity in a city where we cherish our personal bits of space. A ten-foot napkin of grass is like a meadow here where Victorians border the sidewalk. Even cement slab 'backyards' sport potted ficuses. Failing that, a fence keeps your neighbor from seeing bags piled on your garbage cans.

But Mike's building had only a low cement-block wall that anyone could leap. There were even two steps up to the top.

Beyond them a narrow path led to an alley. Alleys lead to streets. The burglar's highway!

Slowly, the chill of the night invaded my clothes. The wind sifted between the buildings, and it struck me that the person who managed to break into Mike's apartment, who turned on the gas full force, had stayed there in the apartment while it filled to the edge of explosion.

Did I *know* that?

Close enough. Too close.

He had been in the apartment with me.

He'd been watching me as I came in, as I tried and tried to open the window. Then, in those few seconds I'd had my head outside, he'd shot behind me and leapt out onto the garbage can. Like a serious pro. Or a desperate amateur.

I shivered. Spitting on your grave, Dad called it, that nauseous near-disaster feeling.

What could he have been after that was so vital? Did he turn on the gas and then search? Figure he'd grab and run and have the explosion cover his exit?

Did I even near-to-know that? Not hardly.

Still, I needed to get back in there and find out.

Get into the place filled with gas.

Shit!

I could call the police. I could whirl around three times and make a wish. Same outcome. Except the wish wouldn't laugh.

My body was vibrating from the tension. I needed to do something.

I did what everyone does. I walked back to the sidewalk, stood and checked messages.

No word from Mike. Why hadn't he called? He'd had time to buy a phone. Marin County wasn't the Sahara; they have stores there. Right across the street from the ferry dock! He could have—

But there was a text. From my agent. Two production companies had new contracts with analgesic makers. '*Send your new video. Pain patches are hot (or cold!)! They need dashes, crashes and crutches! 45 secs.*'

I texted back: *i.e. break a leg? . . . Will do.*

*Send by end of week.*

*Sure thing.*

*Could resurrect your career.*

Resurrect!

*Got it.*

At any time doing a commercial is huge. But now, since my last gig, a movie for which I'd been the stunt coordinator on a disaster of a stunt sequence, no director would want to see *Darcy Lott* on the back of a stunt coordinator's chair, on a casting list of stunt doubles, on the roll of the final credits. I had about as much chance of finding stunt work as did a vat of cottage cheese.

Other stunt doubles might need a commercial, but no one needed it as much as I did.

Video by the end of the week . . . Forty-five seconds is an eternity when every one of them is a shot of you. The prep alone . . . I'd need a camera crew. Maybe one really good guy could handle it. Mike had already done the wire videos. Could I use one of them? Nope. Too short. Not right. But Mike? Yeah, Mike.

If Mike was here.

If he could be safe here.

If I could find the guy attacking him.

I checked the phone again. Zip. But I'd told Mike to leave his number on the zendo landline. The line, I now remembered, with the unreliable message service. Leo and I had intended to get it fixed. Deferred maintenance, electronic style.

I looked around for Mike's grumpy neighbor. Not in sight. It amazed me no one had called the fire department. Even the neighbor. Maybe they figured once the gas was turned off . . . Who knew? The onlookers across the street were already gone and I was standing alone in front of a house still too gassy to go back into for another half-hour at least.

The smell of tomato and garlic wafted down the street. Half an hour to kill – easy choice.

The Haight was a district I hadn't visited much. When I was a kid, it was already over the hill. Going there was like wearing your mother's clothes. Or your mother's memories. I'd heard Mom light up talking about it 'in the day' when it was all free love and music.

Before I could order my pizza slice, my phone rang. John, the cop. I let him go to message as I downed the last of my slice of anchovy and black olive, then checked. 'Darcy, it's almost ten. Why aren't you home? I called your landline. Call me.'

As if!

Text from Gary: *Beware! John – ants in pants. Wants to bitch about me.*

I smiled. Mike excepted, life was normal in the Lott family.

# FOUR

All lights were out in Mike's apartment when I got back. The windows were open. But no one was lowering my brother's belongings to the street. So, all to the good. I walked into the building, eased up the few steps to Mike's door and pushed it open. Had I left it unlocked? Possible when I ran out of the gassy place. Had the guy upstairs? Or someone else . . .

Slithering an arm around, as if I were embracing the door jamb, I flicked on the light, jumped back, waited, and felt a welcome rush of foolish-feeling as the door clattered against the wall. Mike's upstairs neighbor hadn't been alarmed when someone broke in and nearly blew up the building. He wasn't likely to notice me now.

The windows were open but the place still held the odor of gas. I'd been so caught up by the smell here earlier that I'd overlooked the shambles. The place had been tossed. Tan corduroy sofa cushions littered the floor. Drawers had spit out their contents – white undershirts, blue briefs. A red rag oval rug had been pulled up and tossed to the side so it lay against the couch. A framed picture had ended up face down on the floor, bare nail marking its spot on the wall.

Mike's a jeans and T-shirt guy, though he does have at least one nice suit and a couple of sweaters like any guy with three sisters and a mother. He cleans up well.

But the clutter was not homogenous. There were jeans – newish jeans, jeans worn at the knee, ones ripped at the knee, at the butt. A herd of socks. Sweaters, sweatshirts. Men's clothes, women's clothes.

Did Mike have a roommate? Or was the regular tenant a woman? Cross-dresser? *What do you know?* I couldn't know that, not now.

And it looked like the burglar hadn't either. But that hadn't slowed him down.

He'd plowed through, tossing detritus to the sides as he searched for . . . what?

I stood, back to the door, trying to eyeball the place as he had. What had he been after?

If that thing was big, he would have spotted it right off.

If it was the type of object kept in a specific place, he'd have gone straight there.

If it belonged in a drawer, that's what would have been opened. He'd have grabbed it and left. Or shoved the drawer in to check a lower one. He would not have closed those drawers carefully, completely. He would have left them askew, just as they were now.

The interior wall sported a built-in hutch with a china cabinet on top and three drawers beneath. I pulled the top drawer the rest of the way open and found a round plastic container, which might once have held hummus, but now was home to three quarters, a bunch of pennies, a zipper pull – I was guessing a no-longer-closing jacket or pair of pants was on the floor somewhere. A parking receipt that told me someone parked in an unmentioned location for forty-eight minutes the day before yesterday. A tiny notepad with edges that had seen cleaner, uncurled days held something written by an iffy ballpoint pen. Deep lines at the top marked where the writer had tried, with middling success, to get the ink flowing. I couldn't tell how close to success he'd come. *Seren *5 Gate.*

*Seren S5 Gaté? Seren K5 Gaté?*

I'd worry about that later. Next to it there was a small abalone shell, the kind that had once been tourist ashtrays before ashtrays held death, a grocery receipt, and a ratty Giants baseball ticket. If the tenant had had a garbage can, this drawer would have been empty.

The tenant? Because . . . Mike would never save a zipper pull. He wouldn't fool himself that he'd get a zipper repaired. He'd toss the jacket and replenish.

I pocketed the lot, including the abalone shell, which strained the seams of my jacket, and moved on to the second drawer. Socks. A phone book – virtually a museum item! I scanned the front and back cover for jotted phone numbers. Copied down both, though neither was familiar. Two framed posters of the Golden Gate Bridge.

I reached for the bottom drawer.

The outside door banged open. Clatter filled the hallway. Men's voices reverberated. Fists rattled the apartment door.

'Yes?' I called, not opening it.

'We just got here. Sorry. Sorry.' High-pitched voice. Border state rasp. Western Pennsylvania? West Virginia?

'My plane got held up. Some problem over Utah. I shoulda been here hours ago. Airlines! Hey, they got one job, ya know? Fly from A to B, ya know? How hard—' Him I figured for Jersey or New York.

Western Penn mumbled something. Jersey laughed.

I pulled the door open.

The two, both locked-in-the-basement white – one tall, fat, with wiry brown halo, his cohort short, thin, bald and quivering – reached behind for their rolling duffle bag handles and started forward.

'Hey, hold up! I haven't invited you in.'

The big guy flapped a letter at me.

'Reservations. Paid.'

'For here?' For a place someone tried to blow up just hours ago? 'I don't think so.'

If there were a Geek Boutique on Haight, these two would have been prime customers. The big one sported a bigger-yet shirt, size many-X, in faded blue and yellow plaid. Army green chinos. Birkenstocks with socks. The little one wore a blue shirt, dark blue pants, blue windbreaker, all ironed. He could have worked for the post office.

I was peering under the big guy's arm, around the great orb of his gut, to see his friend. It was like conversing with a mastiff and a Pekinese.

'Look!' The letter was flapping like a bird against the wind.

Still blocking the door, I looked. I pointed to the address. 'Upstairs.'

The mastiff grunted.

I caught him before he could reverse his duffle. 'That apartment, is it Airbnb?'

'Hacker hotel.'

'What?'

'Tech Meet.'

'Greek for Geeks.'

'What?' I grabbed his arm. 'Explain.'

'We booked spaces. We heard "come early, get best spot". Anyone else here?'

I remembered the man I'd warned about the gas. 'One.'

'Well, that's OK. The ad said there's one bedroom, bunk, and single. Guess we'll have to bunk. The guys who roll in tomorrow'll get the couch and blow-up in the living room. You end up doing your interfacing there—'

'On their couch and blow-up?'

'Yeah, I guess.'

'And it's legal?'

He shrugged. 'We paid.'

The front door opened again. A woman stepped in and stared at me like I was in the wrong cage in the zoo.

'And you?' I said to her. 'Are you here for the hackers hotel, too?'

'Huh?' She was still staring. The two men turned and checked her out. 'Bad flight?' the small man asked. 'Did you get caught in the delay?'

'Yeah. Right.'

'You need help with your luggage?'

'Huh?'

'Did your luggage make it?'

'No.' She gave her head a shake. 'Sorry. I'm really out of it. It was a lousy flight. My bags are probably still sitting in Dallas. I'm spaced. And starved. Is anything open around here?'

She looked out of it. Long tangle of brown hair, tight T-shirt half out of her jeans, one of those many-pocketed tan cotton vests that used to hold fishing gear but are now more likely to sport phone, wallet and keys. She had the potential to be pretty, but now she just looked wiped out.

'They said there'd be food in the apartment. I'm Tom,' the small man said.

'Heather.'

The other guy didn't offer a name.

'You need to borrow my toothbrush, Heather?' Tom asked.

'Good night,' I said, reaching for the door.

'Yeow, you get tossed?' Heather snaked around the big guy

to stare into the mess of the room. 'I heard about home invasions here. That come down on you?' She stuck her head in, brushing my face with her hair. 'You live alone here?'

I laughed. After the events of the day, laughing felt real good, like a visit to 'normal.' 'No. I'm just collecting some stuff for my brother here.'

'Where's your brother?'

'Out of town.'

'How long will he be gone?'

'Couple days.'

'Where'd he go? I mean, it's hardly worth leaving home for a couple days.'

'You're doing that.'

'Yeah.' She pulled up a smile. 'Guess you're right.'

In another city, another age, they might have wondered why I'd chosen near midnight to root through the belongings of my untidy sibling, but none of them did. I put a hand on Heather's shoulder and eased her back out of the doorway. 'There've been some problems here. Gas leak. If you guys notice anything odd, give me a call, OK?' I gave them my number; they keyed it in.

'OK, goodnight, Heather, Tom, um. Sorry, I didn't get your name?'

'Boots.'

'Boots?'

'For Subhuti.'

'As in the *Diamond Sutra*?'

'Yeah, that one.' And the mastiff named for the Buddha's Diamond Sutra disciple stomped up to the hacker hotel.

I wondered about Subhuti. What unwelcome names had his parents bestowed on his siblings? Or had raising one infant exhausted their whimsy? Or . . . or . . . or was this just a chance to see my own whimsy of thoughts as passing bubbles in a stream that momentarily seemed to be myself?

Mike's apartment; I should . . .

With sudden finality I knew it was too late, in too long a day, to discern any pattern in this clutter. Tomorrow, in the light, I'd check out the surely empty closet. I locked up, walked out, looked around for the car, and remembered it was half a mile away in Golden Gate Park.

'Seemed like a good idea at the time,' I muttered to myself as I slogged up the block and turned west on Haight.

The street still had life, but it had a used feeling, like red wine in a nearly empty glass with old lipstick smudges around the rim. Or like a guy in a cheap 49ers jacket, heaped against a store wall, asking for a denomination he could no longer pronounce. In the park the homeless would be checking spots in the bushes, eyeing new ones if the cops – or bigger, tougher, younger homeless – had rousted them from their last nests. They'd be sleeping with one eye on the next chance, hoping it wouldn't be them.

I picked up my pace, hoping it wouldn't be me. It was late to go into the park but the hour wasn't going to get earlier. If I left the Honda till morning I might as well not bother.

Cars sped by, heading back toward downtown. Headlights startled my eyes and were gone.

Footsteps slapped the macadam walkway behind me.

They weren't behind me a minute ago.

I picked up my pace, almost loping now. I didn't want to run. Not yet.

He – surely, he – matched my pace.

The car was a block's worth ahead. I unslung my pack, felt inside it as I ran. Keys hung from a clasp. I pulled them outside but did not unclasp.

Headlights shone on the empty path, flickered off the bushes, the trees. Snatches of song splattered and were gone. The wind off the Pacific blew wet in my face. It's cold this close to the ocean.

The car was on a side road. Dark. Empty. No reason for traffic. I held my breath, listened hard. He was still behind me. Matching my pace. Which meant he was in better shape than the average homeless guy. If he caught me he'd have something left in the tank.

The footsteps were louder, heavier, suddenly slower. I thought I heard panting but I wasn't about to slow down to find out.

I shot into a sprint, running all out for the car, keys jangling in my hand.

My foot hit something – macadam bulge? I lurched. Caught myself, shot forward.

The car was in view, low, white. I jostled the keys to get the door key in position. I could feel my pace slowing. Hear his feet coming fast. Damn, Mike's car, so old it still had keys. A newer model and I could have beeped and been—

But I wasn't! Focus! This moment!

I skidded to a stop, jammed the key in the lock, turned it, pulled it free and yanked open the door and flung myself inside. I clicked the lock closed.

Then, only then, I stared out the side window, expecting to see a face glaring in at me. But there was nothing. Just bushes, trees and dark. Flash of headlights in the distance through the trees.

I almost wondered if I had made it all up.

But I hadn't.

*What do you know?*

For some reason someone had followed me, and someone had stopped. But that someone now knew what I was driving. Or sitting in.

Warily, I turned the key in the ignition and pressed in the clutch. If the engine had been dead I wouldn't have been surprised. If it had blown up? But it turned over as easily as if it had been sitting happily in a warm garage.

I sighed. All I wanted now was to turn on the heater, drive downtown to my room above the zendo and wriggle into bed.

After I had checked the zendo landline for Mike's message.

# FIVE

I can't swear if anyone was tailing me, but by the time I got home he sure wasn't. I've rolled junkers, done a transfer from the back of a hog to a convertible. I've handled spin-outs on canyon roads. If I couldn't lose a tail in city traffic, I shouldn't be calling myself a stunt driver.

I did eyeball the shadows before I hoisted myself out of the car in front of the zendo. Pacific Avenue was empty. Then, as close to quietly as I could manage, I eased past the little brass plaque announcing 'The Barbary Coast Zen Center' and into the building. The set-up here is meditation hall, *dokusan* (formal interview) room and kitchen on the first floor; two rooms and bath upstairs on either side of the landing, each big enough for a futon, dresser and one other piece of furniture, in Leo's case a writing desk. In mine a trunk holding my 'set bag' so, should I get a last-minute gig, I can grab and run.

It can be cold in San Francisco in April when the wind is off the water, which is pretty much always. Particularly in this building, which has no hope of warmth other than from space heaters. I peeled off my jacket, pushed out of my shoes, and whipped into my sleeping bag.

*Tuesday*

At 6.55 a.m., I slipped into the bathroom, still warm from Leo's shower, peeled the clothes I'd slept in directly into the hamper and leapt in the shower.

By 7.20 I was in the courtyard, hitting the wooden clappers three times. Fifteen minutes to zazen! It gives students a little leeway to make it inside the zendo and settle on their zafus before the abbot enters.

At 7.35, Garson-roshi stepped into the morning-dim zendo. The timekeeper rang a bell as Leo bowed to the altar and then took his seat to the left. Sitting on a cushion, facing the wall, I heard the bells, the soft groan of the floorboards under Leo's feet, the swish as he tucked the bottom of his silk *okesa* under the robes beneath it. There are times, plenty of them, when sitting without moving, seeing thoughts without getting caught in them is hard. This morning, though, it was like coming home. I sat, felt my breath moving, heard the buses, the trucks on Columbus Avenue half a block away, the muted tinkle of glass, the birds doing their morning mad-chirp-and-dead-stop.

When the final bell rang I stood, bowed to my zafu and to the room, thus connecting my silent meditation with life in the world, and walked out.

It's been said that when the water in a pond is still, you can see clearly to the bottom. *Seren*5 Gate.*

*The Book of Serenity?* If that little pad had been in Leo's room, or even mine, it would make perfect sense. *Book of Serenity, case 5.* Koan 5. Why would Mike, or the regular tenant, refer to a Buddhist teaching paradox? The Book of Serenity was a collection of koans, not easy reading. Not the kind of thing you page through on the checkout line. *Hey, Mike, did you get interested in Zen and neglect to mention it to me?*

*Or did you sublet from someone I've heard of, or met?*

What was case 5? I could run upstairs and find out.

Or I could get my morning espresso and then run and find out. I headed out the door across the courtyard to the sidewalk and turned toward Renzo's Caffe.

If a sliver of sun had not pierced the fog, I would have passed right by the Honda and into Renzo's. I would not have spotted the crack in the windshield – not till later, anyway.

I veered across the street to eye the damage. The windshield had been fine last night when I left it.

'Wow! You sure pissed off someone!'

I jumped.

Behind me, pressing in toward the windshield, as if I was merely an impediment to his scoop, was Roman Westcoff. The reporter might not have been the last person I wanted to see, but he rated high. The guy was tall, thin in the way people who view food as mere fodder, and are muscle-avoidant. Now his head hung over my shoulder like the shade on a goose-necked lamp. Even his nose thrust forward, and the little knob on the end all but twitched.

'Getting this fixed is going to set you back three or four hundred easy.'

'True.' The least of my problems.

'Who'd do that to you?'

*To me!* 'Why think it was a person doing it, not an accident?'

'See that circle there in the middle. Mallet-head'll fit it perfect.'

'Perfect*ly*,' I said, because the chance to correct a reporter's grammar doesn't come every day. And because I needed to divert him. 'What are you doing here? Hoping we'd start zazen an hour late?' Westcoff had once spent what looked like the most uncomfortable forty minutes cross-legged on a cushion in the history of Buddhism.

'So . . .?' He was still eyeing the windshield.

'So, Westcoff, what brings you here before breakfast? I don't see you as a morning person.'

He pulled his phone out of a sagging pocket in his tweed jacket. 'Your brother . . .'

*Oh shit!*

'. . . the cop . . .'

*Whew!*

'I need to get a hold of him.'

'Because?' Not that I was planning to stand in Westcoff's way. John had battled the police brass, and irritated pretty much every sworn officer in the city at one time or another. He was a master of stonewalling. In Westcoff's eyes, stonewalling was a sign of guilt, and his mission was to discover the source of that guilt. He was desperate for that one scoop that would catapult him onto the staff at the *Chronicle*. Westcoff vs. John: both used to firing the questions; both loath to give up a hint, much less a lead. I could sell tickets to that.

Minimally it would keep them both out of my hair. Was that what John was calling about last night?

'I've got a couple questions.'

I moved away from the car and made a come motion. 'Questions about . . .?'

'His, uh, associates.'

John's cop buddies? Friends? 'Who are . . .?' This could be fun.

'Hey, I'm already giving you more than you need. Where is he?'

'You don't have his address? You an investigative reporter?'

'Not there.'

'He's not home or not opening the door to you?'

'Not there. Trust me.'

'Not at Mom's?'

'Mom's?'

Damn!

Westcoff grinned. As well he should have.

I gave in. If Westcoff drove out to Mom's she'd invite him in, give him coffee, and make him feel welcome every time he was out by the ocean. By the end of the month he'd be living there. 'I'll call John.'

'Westcoff,' I said when John picked up. 'He was waiting for me when I got out of zazen.'

'If you'd called me back last night—'

'Call him!'

'Ask him what he wants.'

'Call him or he'll be at Mom's door.'

To Westcoff, I said, 'John'll call you in an hour.'

That was my second mistake.

A reporter with an hour to kill is like a bunch of ants with a new entry hole.

I hadn't intended to go back into the zendo building, but hurried across the courtyard, opened the door and said to Westcoff, 'See you!'

'Hang on. Is Mr Garson here?'

*Mr* Garson! 'I'll check. Wait here.'

I checked. Leo is glad to talk dharma with anyone; not that that was likely to be Westcoff's focus. Leo would be perfect to divert Westcoff from the windshield, from discovering that the car belonged to Mike, to splattering me with questions about Mike, to becoming a nuisance, a hindrance, a serious danger to me and to finding the culprit.

Not that it mattered, because Leo was out.

I dawdled in the bathroom, trying to create a plan, but Westcoff hovering outside stifled that. What I needed was in Mike's apartment. What I needed before that was to get rid of Westcoff. I grabbed my pack and headed downstairs. 'Not here. But you're welcome to wait in the courtyard.'

'Nah. I'll tag along with you.'

'I'm in a hurry.'

'Where to?'

I might as well have been spreading sugar by the ant hole. 'Sweatshop. You want to come work out. It's hip-hop day. I can get you a spot in the middle of the line so you can follow the steps.'

He suspected the truth, but hated the idea of hustling to the last place he wanted to enter, and then having to haul himself back because he'd have left his car here.

'OK,' I said. 'Let your body rot. Muscles go to ash. Skin hang off your bones like wet laundry. You know what they say: "Lose your tone, lose your bone." Class doesn't start for fifteen minutes. If we hustle we can still make it. You in?'

He tapped a finger on pen. Considering. He knew, really knew, I was lying, but he didn't know why. He could tag along nagging me. But the cost . . . 'I'll have an espresso and catch you later, Lott.'

'A month ago you didn't know my friend Renzo existed. Now you're parking yourself in his café?'

'Hey, he sees me as a source.'

'Ditto, right?' Westcoff was no fool. Genial Renzo was the proud collector of all things San Francisco. He was born less than a mile from this spot and never lived farther away. He knew everyone and what everyone else said about them. He was the Google of names, the Amazon.com of whatever you needed, and who could get it for you. He'd take whatever Westcoff said and slot it into his collection.

I laughed.

The last laugh though was on me, sort of. Westcoff wasn't going to give up entirely. He'd saunter to his car and prowl the path to the Sweatshop. If he didn't spot me racing up the hill to the gym, he'd wonder why I was so intent on losing him. What was I hiding? So I headed across Columbus, through Chinatown, up Nob Hill to the studio, just as he was chugging his Fiat up the panting-hard-in-first-gear street.

I was tempted to flip him off as I headed inside. I restrained. I waited until he was out of sight, then whipped out, through an alley, down the next street, and into another alley lest he circle back. Much as he might have wanted to, driving right back up the first-gear hill is asking a lot of a little car. I waited though, back to the wall in the alley, eyeing the street, planning my wide, zigzagged loop back past the zendo to the spot where I'd left Mike's car.

Most likely Westcoff's turning up today was a bad sign. For John, if the reporter was eyeing him, even as an auxiliary source on some police story, no good would come from this. Or for me. If Westcoff was not nose-to-the-scent already, then he had time on his hands. It wouldn't take much for him to sniff the new, intriguing scent of The Brother Found, as the papers had called Mike, and be on my heels and in my hair.

After a full, ten minutes, I ran downhill into the edge of Chinatown, cut right toward downtown where 'motion in stillness' traffic precludes tailing any pedestrian, cut down a flight of steps that substituted for a sidewalk, back through the tunnel into Chinatown, over a pedestrian walk and into the Barbary Coast.

All that, just to find Roman Westcoff standing by the Honda's windshield just where I'd left him.

# SIX

'Is this your brother's car?' Westcoff sounded so outraged I had to laugh.

'No.' I could have told him the truth, but Westcoff with any connection to Mike could only mean: bad. I unlocked the driver's door and slid in.

'White Honda. The car your brother Gary bought for Mike when he came home?'

True, but I didn't admit that either.

A couple years after Mike vanished, Gary was the plaintiff's attorney suing a Cadillac-driving coffee magnate who ran over a puppy and left the scene. Any first-year law student could have won that case, but Gary managed 'the kind of settlement that would teach this guy how to drive.' When he got the check, Gary took it directly to the Honda dealer and bought the Civic 'for Mike when he gets back.'

At the time it was a sweet grand gesture.

The Honda sat in Mom's driveway waiting for the big day.

Reminding Mom that Mike was still missing.

After a year, someone moved it into the garage.

When Mom's car, displaced into the driveway and battered by the briny ocean winds, sported new patches of rust, when it needed to be jump-started, it reminded her of Mike.

After a while the Honda became a spare ride for Gary, then Gracie and John. When I came to town for a visit, we drove it and told Mike stories.

None of that would I share with Westcoff, and via him the rest of the news-reading public. I stuck the key in the ignition and started the engine.

Westcoff was on the far side of the car, bending over the windshield, pointing frantically at something in the corner.

'*What?*' I mouthed.

He said something.

I wasn't about to get out of the car.

He pointed to the windshield, then to the door. 'Open the window!'

That, I heard. I leaned over and rolled down the handle.

He reached in and opened the door. 'You can't drive with the windshield like that.'

I just stared at him. 'It's a crack. It's not going to break. The biggest danger is you poking at it.'

'What would your brother say?'

'He'd say get out of his sister's car.'

Westcoff sat, settled his feet on the floor, and pulled the door shut after him. '*Your* car?'

'Get out!'

He grinned. It was like having a skunk in the car. I could pull out all my driving tricks, spin him in wheelies fast enough to make him throw up, but he'd be doing it in my car. 'Tell me, Lott, is this Mike's car?'

'I'm not telling you anything.'

He popped the glove compartment and started riffling through.

'Get out of there!'

He grinned, and kept rooting.

I assumed Mike would have tossed in pens and maps and scraps of paper, but the box was nearly empty. Not even sunglasses. One folder. Westcoff was fingering through it, his face in pre-ah-hah! position.

In a minute he'd have the registration.

In another minute he'd be reading Mike's address.

In an hour he'd be over there discovering that Mike didn't live there any more.

By noon he'd be at Mike's apartment in the Haight, gumming up the works.

Which meant I had three hours to get over there, search the apartment and go where that led me.

'You weren't lying.' Westcoff sounded shocked. I was shocked. He was wagging the registration at me.

I raised an eyebrow.

'His sister's car. I thought you were just blowing me off. But, dammit, this is his sister's car. Dr Grace Lott; your sister, right?'

*The car was registered to Gracie? Why would that be?* I said, matter-of-factly, 'Yes.'

'She's the epidemiologist, right?'

Among other things. She's also a notoriously distracted driver, the absent-minded professor of epidemics. When she works she's all work. Gracie's scandalously unreliable about social commitments. No one leaves her a message and truly expects a call back, not in the same week anyway. And, she has her own vehicle. Of all of us Lotts, she is the last one in whose name anyone would register their car. 'Yes, the doctor.'

'So, who would be bashing in her windshield? How come?'

'You know – and I know that you know – I lived out of state for almost the whole time Mike was missing. I didn't have much contact with the family. So, there's a lot of stuff that passed me by, particularly small stuff between siblings. With Gary I missed one of his wives entirely. What I'm saying is, I'm not the best person to ask.'

He shrugged, a little smile on his eager face. 'I'll ask her.'

I hesitated only momentarily. But you can have a lot of thoughts in a moment. I love Gracie. We've had each other's back; we've had good times. John excepted, I wouldn't choose to sic Westcoff on any of my siblings. But no one's cleaner than Gracie. Other than parking tickets for all the times she's gotten caught up in meetings, distracted by calls, or just decided to walk around the block and ponder, there is no black mark. No dirt.

I could call and warn her. If she picked up her messages. But, even so, she's not focused enough to be a consistent liar. No, better to just let this play out. I turned to Westcoff and said, 'Knock yourself out.'

He was barely on the curb when I shot into the street and was gone. He'd be looking up Gracie's number, waiting while it rang, being put on hold by her assistant, listening to phone music, listening to Carmela's explanation of why Dr Lott was not available at this time and would barely be for the rest of the day, and finally he'd be telling her to have Gracie call him back.

By then I'd be in Mike's apartment.

# SEVEN

Google saved me. I should have checked the *Book of Serenity* before I left the zendo. I would have, had it not been for Westcoff and the cracked windshield (which was holding up just fine, thank you very much!)

At not quite ten-thirty, I wriggled Mike's Civic into a space about two inches longer than the car, at the end of Mike's block. It took me seven tries and a wee ride over the SUV bumper in front, but in a district where many eyelids were just now flickering open, no one was going to complain.

I pulled out my phone, did a search, and found *Book of Serenity, One Hundred Zen Dialogues.* Case 5: A monk asked Qingyuan, 'What is the meaning of Buddhism?' Qingyuan said, 'What is the price of rice in Luling?'

Traditionally a student is given a koan to hold loosely in her mind. *Ponder* is too direct a term because the strength of the koan is that it forces the student to break through the wall of thought to understanding. We Zen types like to ponder, to discuss, ruminate. Letting go of thought is like letting go of skin. We fight, fight, and only when we're overwhelmed do we let go.

*What is the meaning of Buddhism?* we all want to know.

I could imagine asking Garson-roshi in *dokusan.*

Leo, in his black robes, sitting on his cushion in the formal interview room, facing me on my own cushion and saying, 'What is the meaning of life? What is the Truth? We want to know that, too, right?'

Me, sheepishly nodding.

Him saying: 'And what will the Dow be at the closing tomorrow?'

Me: 'If we knew that, we'd be rich.'

Him smiling. 'Traders devote their lives to predicting—'

Me: 'But they can't know.'

Leo snapping his fingers.

*Now! Just this!*

*Don't delude yourself.*

Fine and good for Leo and me. For Zen students who haul themselves to the zendo before work in the morning and sit facing a blank wall. *What is the meaning of Buddhism?*

Mike? Mike might give a passing thought to a koan, but why would he note it down? If he did give thought to a koan, it would be to one of the better-known ones like the sound of one hand clapping, or the tree falling in the forest. This one, though, would be an odd choice. Faced with, *What is the price of rice in Luling?* he'd probably decide to go out for Chinese food.

A pickup drove slowly by, driver eyeing me questioningly. I shook my head. He hit the gas, nearly stalled out, and roared off.

I stared out the window. The sun shone but the street wasn't really awake yet. A woman hurried uphill as if late to get to the streetcar stop. Two thirty-somethings strode by, eyes straight ahead, hands gesturing, leaving a trail of annoyance. 'Neighborhood! Weekend rents! Oughta . . . law.'

The façade of Mike's building was not enhanced by sunlight. The sort-of-white paint was tinted with dirt. Shoes had scuffed the outside steps down to wood and the memory of paint was visible only on the risers. The building was on a slope, the stairs on the upside, a drop to a garage downhill beside it. A clutter of trash had taken up residence in front of the garage door.

I stepped inside. Last night the entry hall had been silent, but now footfalls from above hit the floor like a hailstorm. Voices grumbled. The techies upstairs were here to mingle. They might be dragging themselves up after a long night, or night could still be going on for them.

I unlocked Mike's door . . . and gasped.

Under a pile of blankets on the sofa was a body.

My chest went cold. All the time Mike had been missing, I'd refused to think him dead. When reports of disasters, tall young men killed in accidents, shoot-outs, from freak medical anomalies, I'd gritted my teeth and turned my back. The specter of death was always with me, fear at the ready. I wanted to turn and run now, before I could see what I couldn't bear to see.

The blankets quivered.

The body pushed herself up, looking equally startled.

I was so ridiculously relieved – she looked nothing like Mike

– I nearly laughed. Then, I was just pissed. 'Heather? This isn't part of the hacker deal. This is a private apartment.' Or maybe it wasn't.

She gave her head a shake. 'Sorry. I know. I hoped you wouldn't mind. The guys, you know? They started out serious into Boots's app—'

'Boots, the big guy.'

'Yeah, the one from Jersey. So, like, both of the guys are talking program and production costs and scope of sale and, like, that's fine. But then, you know, guys! The old guy who was already there, Wally, he had a bottle of something and Boots and Tom, they're not drinkers, believe me. But they weren't about to admit that. In no time flat the whole scene morphed into a bunch of high school boys whose parents are away for the weekend. It was gross. Like the Wikipedia illustration for gross.' She'd pushed herself up to sitting, one self-shove per complaint. Now she pulled the blanket off and began folding it. 'Anyway, I'm sorry about breaking in here.'

'How'd you manage that?'

'Wally got keys from whoever lives here. He gave one to the temporary tenant – your brother, right? – and kept the spare. I figured there might be one. I lucked out. I'm sorry. But listen, you can still hear them up there. If the key hadn't worked here I would have crawled to the airport and sat in front of the boarding ramp till the next flight to . . . anywhere. You're not going to call the police, are you?'

'Did you touch anything?'

'Uh-uh. Except the bathroom. I didn't even go in the kitchen or the other room. I was so wiped I just fell on this sofa and didn't move till now.' She looked like she'd been embalmed.

I did a quick scan of the room. She probably hadn't touched anything. Who could tell? She could have filled the drawers with drugs and concealed a couple of AK-47s under the couch and left no clue.

She pushed herself up to standing. I'd have guessed her to be about twenty-three, thin to too-thin and basement-white, in an unhealthy female version of Tom and Boots. If these three were any example, a stalk of celery or a carrot could survive a decade in the Geek Meet. Her tangle of brown hair looked much the same as last night, her T-shirt advertising a band I'd never heard of was scrunched up around her ribs and she had one sock off. She spotted the other, dropped to the floor and began pulling it on.

She was, I noted, a woman in desperate need of coffee. I was one in need of her gone. I pulled out a ten. 'How about getting us coffees and yourself a pastry, whatever this'll buy?'

'Hey,' she snapped, 'I'm not a poor relation. I've got money!'

'Fine. Two pastries, then, and make my coffee a macchiato.' A macchiato is a caffè latte with the shot added last. Renzo sneers at affectations like that. Like strawberry lattes. Like New Yorkers view blueberry bagels.

Heather seemed to be having an internal struggle, but that was her problem.

'What about your brother who lives here? Should I get him coffee, too?'

It was such an ordinary question I smiled.

'I mean, will he be back soon?'

Fingers crossed! 'You never know with brothers, right?'

'Maybe. I grew up with asshole cousins. The difference is you care about your brother.'

She was standing by the door. It took me a moment or two to realize she was waiting for a reply. 'Yeah,' I said. 'Probably more than I should.'

Before she could go on, I ushered her out. What I'd said was true. Another thing I didn't want to think about.

I stood, back to the door, closed my eyes and blocked out thoughts till my mind was clear, then I tried to put myself in the body of the hit-and-run driver, the would-be windshield smasher, the guy who turned the gas and left this whole place to blow up. I'd managed this maneuver in acting classes. But it was a technique more suitable for a class. There the subject is a given – a man asking for directions, a traffic cop, a ballerina missing a shoe. Here it was a question. Still, I closed my eyes and imagined I had just illegally entered. At night. My skin tingled, my gut was tight, teeth jammed together. My breaths came fast and shallow. The room was dark. There were, I recalled, no shades. I wouldn't turn on the light. So, I'm trying to find 'the thing' by streetlight. I'm desperate to get it and get out. The floorboards upstairs are creaking.

Or was that now?

Or both? If it was then, the noise makes the me-intruder edgier. I'm dead still, listening, to the creak, to the cars outside, the burst of chat on the sidewalk. I'm holding . . . something . . . burglar tools?

No. Those are for pros. I'm . . . a one-timer. I'm here for . . . something Mike brought with him when he came here temporarily to house-sit. Something he didn't want to – didn't dare – leave where he was. Because . . .

. . . the attacks had already started. The attacker – I – know where he lives, what he drives.

My eyes snapped open. Of course he knew what car Mike drove. That's how he followed Mike to the pier, how he shifted to me, how he knew which windshield to smash.

If he hadn't already followed Mike here, he followed me.

Whatever he – I – was looking for, if Mike brought it here, it had to be small enough to carry. Something he could bring in without drawing the kind of attention that it ended up drawing.

I was desperate to start looking around. But I stayed put, shutting my eyes again, now imagining my intruder-self leaving the apartment. 'Rewinding' had been the next step in class.

He – I – would have—

Assumption upon assumption! Exactly what was called for in acting class. But here, now . . .?

*What is the price of rice in Luling?* Don't focus on what you can't know. Maybe this koan wasn't for Mike but for me!

I opened my eyes. If Mike brought something with him for safe-keeping, he'd have concealed it. I'd learned my brother's modus operandi after years of childhood conspiring, watching him hide the baggie of pot Mom never searched for, secrete a key in the turquoise vase of dried flowers in the upstairs hall that Mom had won at a school fundraiser, tape a pack of condoms on the top of a door no one ever shut. And there was the time he hid and forgot a pair of rock-climbing shoes he'd bought for my birthday so well I never did find them.

If anyone could find a Mike Lott hiding spot, it was me.

I strode into the kitchen, pulled out the drip pan from beneath the old refrigerator.

Nothing.

Checked the tops of the moldings. Scooted down to eye the underside of the table for papers. Too obvious, anyway.

Just in case, I looked around for a rice canister. But this was not the kitchen of a from-scratch cook.

In the bathroom I pulled the rubber mat up from the tub, unfolded the towels, checked the hem of the shower curtain.

Damn! If I just knew the size of the thing!

Footsteps banged on the stairs outside. I'd been too focused to note whether they were going up or down. Heather? She could wait. Sit on the steps and eat.

I skipped the closet and scanned the rest of the bedroom. Ignored under the bed, bottoms of drawers, places Mike would have been embarrassed to use. I pulled off the smoke alarm. Hiding an item the size of a wad of cash in the battery slot? But no. I traced the top of the door jambs, lifted a floor lamp to check underneath. Ran my fingers around the inside of the shade.

The floorboards were uneven but Mike wouldn't be pulling up the floor in someone else's apartment.

A light fixture hung from the middle of the ceiling, shielded by a thick shade. He could have reached it from a chair. Me? No way. Still, I didn't need to unscrew the shade; I just needed to see if anything was lying in it. I flipped the light switch. Nothing. At least nothing large. But a paper? Cash? Maybe.

I climbed on a chest and from there hoisted myself onto the top of a bookcase next to the door. An insufficiently sturdy bookcase. It took me a full minute of concentration and tiny weight-shifts to steady it. Slowly I turned toward the light fixture, hands against the ceiling to brace myself.

The front door banged open.

How . . .? I had the key Heather had used. How did she—

'Crowd-sourcing is crap. You know, who needs nickels from strangers? Losers, that's who.'

Boots. Subhuti from New Jersey. Strolling into the living room like this was the downstairs annex. Which, apparently, it had morphed into.

'The key is converting power' – this from Tom. 'If you can run the sun through the roof panels into your tank – what used to be your gas tank – you're set. Look, you're never going to use all that—'

'You loco, hombre? You can run your whole house on internet.'

'Your house, hell. Your life, man.'

'Click on the net and watch a guy open his door, turn on the stove – he's got a pot of soup or something there, text his woman to be there in ten minutes, and warm up the shower. His cars are powering up in the garage. Water outside, that's a given, right—'

'The way I see it, it's boundless. Only limitations are small minds—'

'Maybe he's got a, you know, personal pleasure performer and he's powering it up for a little pre-prandial—'

'We have no way of knowing how vast . . .'

If I hadn't been perched on top of a bookcase, I would have laughed. How long had these two assumed they were having a conversation? I would have been more surprised at the parallel monologs if I hadn't grown up with brothers. With Boots and Tom going at it, no wonder Heather needed to escape down here.

I gave the light fixture a visual once-over and, spotting nothing in it but bulbs, lowered myself to the floor. The question was not whether the two in the next room would ask what I'd been doing, but whether they would notice the thump of my landing at all. Much less break verbal stride to ask about it.

'Solar!' Tom sounded like he was in the kitchen. 'Storage! Storage is the bottleneck. Always. Did you read the piece in DT by the guy in Andalusia about chips that make micro look macro? That's tomorrow . . .'

I stood in the bedroom. There was nowhere else to search. I had zip. And nowhere to go from here. I sighed. Then, with the trudge of futility, I adopted the Sherlock Holmes dictum and considered the hiding places I was so sure Mike would have eschewed. I pulled open a dresser drawer for a cursory glance.

And stopped dead.

The underwear in the drawer was definitely not Mike's.

But the handgun nestled in the black lace bra could be.

# EIGHT

I stared at the gun, a nine-millimeter Glock. Not the kind of thing a girl tucks in her bra, not unless she wants to fall flat on her face.

I'd never seen Mike with it. Or any handgun. I couldn't imagine him applying for a permit.

I couldn't imagine him keeping an illegal weapon in his apartment when he was being threatened and might have to call the cops.

If it was Mike's, why was the gun here in the drawer rather than in his pocket when he might need it?

And who wore the lingerie?

If I could find her name and track her down. I could go to her house . . .

Which was just where I was now. This was *her* apartment. If I Googled her and found her address, that address would bring me here.

But, right now, she had to be somewhere else.

If you know you're going away you leave a contact number with a friend or neighbor.

'Wally, upstairs,' I said to Boots and Tom, who were still bantering about business models in the living room, 'is he home?'

'Asleep,' Boots said without looking over. 'The guy in Phoenix already tried that. It bombed.'

'His model differed in distinguishable ways,' Tom insisted. 'For instance—'

'Give me your key.'

He gave.

I took the stairs two at a time, stuck the key in the door and pushed it open. 'Wally!'

A person on the floor wriggled down and pulled his sleeping bag over his head. All that escaped was a tail of blond hair. On the sofa, a bearded, bear-like man groaned and snuggled his face against the back cushions.

If these two were the living room contingent, and Tom and Boots had taken bunks in the bedroom with, presumably, Wally, it was hard to see where Heather might have slept if she hadn't escaped downstairs. How many spaces was Wally renting out? Beds + 1? Beds + 6?

'Wally!'

A man stumbled out of the bedroom, glared at me, and veered to the kitchen. I followed.

I hadn't paid much attention to him yesterday during the gas scare. But now I assessed him, unhindered by subtlety or good manners. The old guy. Probably in his late sixties, he was short, too thin, too bent, too pale. He had too little hair with too little hue to place it as graying brown or blond. The most notable thing about him was his cough. It shook him like a flag. I expected to see him pull out a pack of cigarettes, but he didn't. He clicked on a coffee maker, opened a cabinet door, glared at the hooks hanging from the bottom of the middle shelf – all empty – and without altering his expression turned his head to the sink. It was crammed full, with dishes, stained cups, stainless cutlery, balanced like aerialists in a high-wire routine.

'Gotta get paper,' he said and coughed.

'Plates?'

'Yeah. Cups they'd spill all over.' He picked up a white ceramic cup and began to scrub.

'This is your apartment? You're on the lease?'

'My house. I'm on the deed.'

I looked from the living room back to him. 'I assumed . . . So these guys are here at your invitation?'

'Yeah.'

'And it's OK with your tenant downstairs?'

'Adrienne, no. She hates it. Threatened to call the city or whatever.'

'Did she?'

'Nah. City wouldn't do shit. She knows that. I told her if she didn't like it, she could move.' He coughed. 'Like she's ever going to find another place this close to the park for less than an arm and a leg and all that's between.'

'So she has to put up with it?'

'She can leave for the duration.'

'Where does she go?'

He turned to face me full on. 'Who the hell are you?'

'The one who warned you about the gas last night! Maybe saved your life and building.'

He coughed, as if to demonstrate which of the two was least valuable.

'Where can I find her?'

'Not here.'

I just waited.

'Gone. I don't care where. Gone is gone.'

'You must have some idea. Her clothes are still here. If there was an emergency you have to have a way to contact her, just as a neighbor if not—'

'We're not buddies here. The best thing she's done is leave.'

'So you could have all these guys talking all night?'

'Well, yeah,' he said with honest surprise. 'How do you think I make the payment on this place? On social security? On a pension that would have paid me a few hundred a month if the company hadn't gone bust? But these tech kids, they come four times a year – not the same ones, I mean not the same names, but the same types; they're like a litter of puppies stumbling over each other to get to the teat first. But come noon they'll be gone to their meetings. Come Monday they'll be gone, period, and they will have made my payment for months.'

I thought of Boots and Tom, neither of whom looked like they owned an extra shirt. 'How do they get that kind of money?'

'Investors. Parents. Conferences are a big deal. Once they make it big, cash is like Monopoly money to them. Suddenly they've got wads and they're looking to put hotels on Boardwalk.'

'So your tenant is doing you a favor vacating her flat.'

'She's getting a deal.'

'Look,' I said, exasperated, 'I was born in this city. My brother was a cop here; my other brother's a lawyer here. My sister's a doctor. I know this city. I walked past this place when I was a kid. Probably walked past you—'

'Your point?'

My hands knotted into fists. I took a deep breath and did not call him a hungover pain in the ass. I tried for compassion, but compassion's hard to stir up for the annoying. Still, the effort must have been some use, because my voice was a few notes lower when I said, 'I know the city can't sell out fast enough. Cafes – you used to overhear guys taking painting, reading poetry, women planning murals. Now you get grunts about tax deductions, square footage, bottom line. By end of this decade, your San Francisco will be a museum and Haight Street will become all facades.'

It was hard to say which of us was more surprised: him to hear his take coming from a younger mouth, me to find it at home in my own. Complaint about the changing city was as much a part of local history as the Golden Gate Bridge or 1906 Earthquake. The latest wave was never as genuine as what it washed away. Old-timers on this very block must have bitched and whined 24/7 at the hippie influx in the Summer of Love, the tie-dyed explosion that changed the city and gave it its cachet. Each new wave was a tsunami threatening to drown the locals. Each overwhelmed incarnation glowed brighter in its absence. Repetitive, but true. And suddenly I felt compassion for him, and for me.

I said simply, 'I need to find her.'

'Why?'

'My brother was house-sitting for her. You probably saw him. He looks like me—'

'Taller.'

'Right. He forgot to tell her about a change in plans.' It sounded lame to me.

And apparently to him. 'Oh yeah?'

'That's what he told me.' *When you're lying, keep it brief.* That aphorism from John.

But brief wasn't doing the trick here. Wally stared at me with more focus than I would have guessed possible. He was eyeing me and he was considering. 'How is it Mike knows her?'

*Keep it brief.* I shrugged. 'I don't know.'

'Mike had a change in plans? What plans?'

Frantically I scoured my scraps of knowledge about the woman. Most of what I knew was her underwear. Maybe the zipper pull was hers. Or the abalone shell. Or the baseball ticket. 'He got a call about a ticket switch from tomorrow to tonight. The Giants game.' Were the Giants playing tonight? Were they here or at an away game? If they were in Denver and Wally knew it, I was totally and permanently screwed.

I was not. Wally smiled, though he looked to be moving muscles counterintuitively, 'I think she was headed to the east bay, or maybe Marin or Sonoma.'

Or one of those places old-time San Franciscans view as the greater undifferentiated hinterland.

'Do you have her number?'

'I'll call her. She wants to, she can call you.'

'It's easier if I call her.'

'Easier for you. Like I said, I'll get in touch with her.'

My phone rang. I muttered thanks and raced for the door to take it outside, just about mowing down Heather on the way.

'Thanks a lot!' the voice on the phone said.

# NINE

'You owe me!'

'I know, Gracie. Did Westcoff call you?'

'He threatened to bang on the door if I didn't pick up. You know I don't have time for the phone.'

I pictured her pacing like a dark-haired pixie in a dry square fishbowl, smacking the glass, turning so fast it was like she'd leapt over her reaction and was double-timing to the other side of the bowl. Mike and I can lope for miles. Gary and Gracie sprint, their blue eyes locked on the finish line. Now she'd be charging through the living room, dining room, into the kitchen for something she'd have forgotten by the time she reached the counter. 'How could you sic—'

'Why is Mike's car registered to you?' I said, cutting short the issue of my questionable intentions.

'I don't know.'

'How can you not know? You had to go to the DMV, sign forms, pay money. How—'

'He asked. I did it.'

'And?'

'He was just back here after all those years missing. He asked. I didn't want to poke into anything, you know?'

I nodded at the phone. None of us had wanted to poke. We'd all been walking on breakaway glass, desperate to make Mike's re-entry into the Lott family as smooth as possible. 'I know.'

What I knew – not in the sense that Leo meant, *What do you know?*, but what made sense – was that Mike couldn't or didn't want to register the car in his own name, so he asked the one of us most likely to be so distracted by work that she wouldn't think to question him.

If I asked her now, she'd probably agree. But she was talking about something else. Something about cake.

'What?'

'Can you drop a cake off at Mom's? It's on order at SugarPlum. Just needs to be picked up. I paid.'

Wait! She hadn't called about Westcoff? Ranting about him was just a preamble. She'd called about cake? 'When does Mom need it?'

'Four.'

'This afternoon? Gracie, it's already noon. Couldn't you have given me a little more warning?' I said that last for my own pleasure. If she'd been organized enough to give me warning, she wouldn't need me now. If she'd been less the absent-minded epidemiologist, she wouldn't be Gracie. The only reason she had a house to pace in was because one Christmas the family organized the entire real-estate operation – hunt, buy, and sign. We organized; she paid. The next year's gift was furniture. When it came to children, I told her, she was on her own.

'It's been a bad day.'

That didn't sound like my sister. Her style was a prickle of crises, most with five syllables. 'How so?'

'I'm under the weather.'

'Why don't you leave work early?'

'I'm home.'

'You never take a day off.' This was bad. 'How come you're home?'

'I was too dizzy to drive.'

'Because?'

'I fell.'

'Because?'

'I wasn't paying attention.'

What else was new? If it wasn't a potential epidemic, it wasn't in her range of vision. Her fridge was more often empty than filled. She was renowned for forgetting social events. In the year I'd been back in the city, she'd overshot Mom's house four times – the house she grew up in! Things like that, though, she didn't classify as inattention. So this . . .? 'And . . .?'

'I got hit.'

'By a car?'

'Well, yeah.'

Ignoring that soupçon of sarcasm, I said, 'What exactly happened?'

'I was crossing the street—'

'When?'

'This morning, on the way to work.'

'The street you live on?'

'Well, yeah.'

'At your regular time?' Getting to work on time was one of the few things to which my sister did pay attention.

'Seven twenty, like always. Car smacked me in the back. Threw me onto the curb. I hit my head.'

Omigod! 'Did you go to Emergency?'

'Darcy, I'm a doctor! I called in sick and iced my head. I'm fine. But I forgot about the cake.'

'Did you see the make of the car?'

'As I was flying into the curb?'

Point taken. I was shaking. First Mike, now her. Mike got hit a second time. 'Don't leave your house!'

'I didn't go to work.'

Another point taken. Normally she'd stagger into work even if she was dead. 'Have someone come over.'

'That's what I'm asking *you* to do!'

I swallowed the flock of things I wanted to say – I'd see her soon enough – and went with, 'You want me to get the cake from the bakery?'

'Jeez,' she grumbled. 'Oh, and Darce, don't mention this to Mom. Or anyone. OK?'

'OK. Here's the deal. I'll handle the cake. You call a friend to stay with you . . . No, no, don't protest. I've got all the cards here. You get a friend over to spend the night or I tell John what happened. Got it?'

The last thing I wanted was to toss my brother in this mix. If Gracie'd been in better shape she would have known that.

If she'd been in better shape she would have convinced the bakery to deliver, and never called me at all. I should be grateful to – amazingly – Westcoff. Not that I'd be telling him that.

It was Mike I needed to talk to. I needed to say, *I thought it was just the car he was after, when he smacked the windshield. Just a calling card. But it wasn't the car. It was me, right? Your family. And now Gracie.*

*Did you have any clue . . .?*

But I wouldn't have asked him that. If he'd even considered there could be danger to us, he'd've . . . something.

*What would you have done? Called John?*

I could call John right now.

Calling John was chancing a step into overkill. In no time there would be cronies of John stationed in Gracie's living room, riding shotgun when she went to work. Gracie on the horn to me every hour, bitching. John dogging my steps. Cronies in Mike's Haight apartment. All of them alerting the attacker to lie low, wait them out, and target Mike when he came back.

What I needed was to talk to Mike, have the back-and-forth as we had years ago, as we had a bit since I tracked him down and brought him back. In those couple minutes it had been . . . normal. I wanted to say: *I was worried before, Mike, when it was just you in danger. But now . . . You know how to watch out for yourself. Gracie hasn't a clue. If I told her to watch out, she'd look both ways before taking a single step. For half an hour she'd become a parody of* looking out. *Then she'd forget the whole game. I was worried before, but this is a whole different level of dread.*

If I said all that, Mike would burst out of his nest of safety, wherever that was, race back to the city and double the danger.

More to the point, there was no way to reach him.

But I had to *do* something. I couldn't surveil Gracie's house. I wasn't even getting anywhere watching Mike's place.

*When you don't know what to do, do the next thing.* Leo.

The cake!

I started toward the car.

Was the guy watching me? He might already know where every one of Mike's relatives lived, but I'd be damned if I'd get in the car and lead him to Mom's. I walked to the streetcar stop.

An hour and forty-five minutes later, having been on two lines that went underground and out again, I knocked on Mom's door.

'I can't stay,' I said, holding out the cake box.

I so wanted to go in, sit at the kitchen table where we all gathered to talk, plan, divvy up, and work things out. I wanted to walk on the beach with Mom and Duffy, look out at the fog sitting on the water, and pour out the things I couldn't say. I couldn't tell her about the threats to Mike. I couldn't let her know about the attack on Gracie. I couldn't say anything without withholding. Suddenly I felt more isolated than I ever had, like I was in that square fishbowl and the rest of the world outside.

I bent down and scratched Duffy behind his perky black ears. He leapt up on my unstable lap and rubbed his head against my chest. He never does anything so lap-doggy.

I gave him a thank-you squeeze, muttered, 'Got to run,' and did just that.

I barely made it back in time for evening zazen. Even a fast run along The Great Highway next to the beach, and catching the M car on the far side was not speedy transit. *They also serve who only stand and wait* could be the MUNI motto at rush hour. I jumped off at Carl and Cole, ran the couple blocks to Mike's car, eyeballing the empty-looking house as I passed, and drove through rush hour across town. *They also serve who only sit and wait.*

I sat zazen. I ordered pizza, left Leo half, took mine and a bottle of water, drove to Mike's, parked across the street. Sat and waited, eyed the growing shadows beside stairs to front doors, the garbage walkways between houses, checked all the mirrors Mike had set up in the car. If the guy was keeping watch on Mike's now, I did not spot him.

Tom, Boots and Heather dragged themselves up the stairs before I finished the second slice. They stumbled back out halfway through my bottle of water. And while I was vacillating whether to use Mike's bathroom, they came back. The light went on upstairs. It dimmed. It was 9.15!

Wally did not come or go.

At 9.30 I exited the car, made a run for McDonald's bathroom line, and circled back via the park panhandle, stood shivering in the shadow of a staircase across the street for so long that I wondered if the assailant had given up.

It wasn't till I got back to the zendo that I noticed the message from Gary. 'Call me. No matter how late.'

It was midnight. I called.

# TEN

My middle brother answered my call before I could speak. 'Hey, Darce, you want a car for a while?' he said, as if we were chatting at lunch. It's a skill of his – Mr Chipper, alert, ready to handle your every legal need, regardless of the hour.

'Thanks, Gar, but . . .' I almost said I've got Mike's Honda. But I didn't want to get into anything concerning Mike. 'I'm good as is.'

'How about the Aston?'

'Wow. I thought you got that baby to show off to clients.'

There was a muffled sound of him clearing his throat.

'OK,' I backtracked, 'I assume you procured it to reinforce your reputation for success by letting clients see your half-a-million-dollar ride.'

'I got it used.'

I laughed. My brother so straddled 'hot-shot lawyer' and 'man of the people,' he was lucky he didn't split himself straight up the crotch.

'Listen, Darce, I'm really pressed for time here. You want it or not?'

'I said no.'

'It's parked across the street from my office, on the side street. I'll leave the keys with Akbar.'

'As I said, I don't need it.'

'It's right outside. Tank nearly full.'

'I said—'

'Take it.'

'Why?'

He hesitated, something he's trained himself never to do. *Indecision suggests incompetence.* Gary had his aphorisms, too. I could *see* him in this unfamiliar state, sitting in his wooden swivel chair in the bay window overlooking Columbus Avenue, the streetlight shining over his shoulders, sitting, but his mind pacing as determinedly as Gracie.

'There's been a problem in my garage across the street. I've got to clear out the cars. Akbar's found garages for two of them. I'm driving the Beemer. So that leaves the Aston.'

'Problem in your garage?'

'This is just between us?'

How had I become the repository of secrets in this family? 'Of course.'

'There's grease all over the floor.'

'Don't you lock your garage?'

'Long story. Point is the grease. Thick. I don't know what it is exactly, but I just about killed myself when I stepped on it. Went sliding back out the door and into the street. Bus missed me by inches. Driver freaked, just about hit the median. You don't expect a body to come flying at you mid-block in the dark. If there'd been passengers they'd have been flung like loose luggage. I'm telling you, I shot out of the garage like something out of a slapstick movie.' He made a sound that might have been a forced laugh. 'I have to get the cars out of there and get the floor dealt with. I've got a settlement hearing on the Converse case in the morning. I can't spend the night trying to back cars out through the grease on to Columbus and praying no one smacks me halfway downtown.'

*Could have been killed.* I was barely breathing. *Be careful*, I yearned to say. But that's just what he was being and it wasn't enough. 'Get the tires changed,' I forced out. 'Check under the hood, under the body. Make sure they're clean. Get them towed.'

'I don't think—'

'Towed, Gary! You're asking me a favor. You do this for me. Clear?'

'OK. I'll tell Akbar. But that means he'll be occupied when you get here. The keys will be in his right-hand drawer.'

I nodded. But Gary had already hung up. If I'd been paying him by the tenth of the hour I'd have been glad to skip the goodbyes.

# ELEVEN

*Wednesday*

I woke up thinking: He knows where we live. He's telling us he knows; he can come back any time. Gracie and Gary were lucky . . . this time. I was lucky he'd only smashed the Honda's windshield outside here yesterday morning. Mike could have been in his apartment when it blew up. I was sweating. I felt like I was going to pop out of my skin. I had to do something.

There were no leads to follow. Nothing to do. Everywhere was a dead end.

Call John? I'd promised Mike not to; promised Gracie, promised Gary. The price for that call would be enormous. Never again would I be trusted with a secret. Or considered reliable, or competent. John would be all over me. But he'd still have time to berate Gracie and Mike for not calling him themselves, and Gary for that and for not insisting the rest of us call him. As for Mike . . . if he'd left me a working phone number, assuming he was not working at capacity just calling me . . . but I couldn't unravel that now.

But John could have men keeping watch on Gracie, Gary's garage, Mike's apartment, me. Mom's. He could . . . how much could he really do?

*When all things are dead ends, do the next thing.*

Was that a Zen koan or did I dream it? Whatever, I sat morning zazen hoping that an empty mind would lure the right answer. Then I downed an espresso at Renzo's Caffe.

Wally had promised to call Adrienne, his tenant and Mike's 'landlady.' Maybe he had. Maybe not. Maybe he'd reached her and she'd promised to call me. Maybe not. Same difference. I'd waited long enough. At 8.30 I called Wally.

'Wally?'

'Yeah?'

'Darcy Lott, Mike's sister. I was there yesterday.'

'Yeah, so?'

'Has Adrienne called?'

'Nah.'

'When did you call her?'

'I don't know. Sometime after you left.'

*Obviously.*

'Right after?'

'When I got to it.'

Maybe. 'Did you tell her to call me?'

'Listen. You hear that racket here? It's like that 24/7. These geeks chug those wake-up drinks, you know? They're speeding all the time. Day, night, no difference. They're nattering about their apps and crap. Banging pans on the stove, slamming cabinets. I've got a carpenter on stand-by; we're on first names, the carpenter and me.'

'I'll do it,' I said matching his irritated tone. 'What's Adrienne's last name?'

'Ferente.'

'Her phone number?'

'Whadaya think, I'm your personal assistant here?'

'I think a landlord has his tenant's phone number, so he can call her to complain.'

He coughed, but I had the feeling it was a forced sound to cover the fact that I'd hit on the truth.

'What do you want with her?'

'She sublet or lent her apartment to my brother. On short notice. How come? Do you know?'

'Nah.' He could have been a cop with that 'we ask, you answer' tone. 'That it? You going to ask her anything else?'

With luck, yeah. 'Should I?'

'Here. Four one five—'

'Is that her landline?'

'Yeah, so?'

'Give me her cell.'

'Why would I need that when she's right downstairs? That all?'

Before I could answer he'd hung up.

I Googled Ferente. I Whitepaged. No 'A. Ferente' per se in the city, though a dozen close spellings. I dialed Wally again.

'Yeah?'

I could barely hear him over a mishmash of electronic, kitchen electric, and shouts that could have been encouragement or warning.

'Adrienne's last name. Ferente – F-E-R-E-N-T-E? You sure?'

'I'm going to go deaf by morning but I'm not losing my eyesight. She signs her checks every month. I look 'em over – tenants short on cash, you never know what they'll do. No signature. No amount. Signature on the memo line. All sorts of garbage. They—'

'Was Adrienne short of cash?'

'Nah, she has a good deal. She knows that.'

*So why go into this riff?* But I didn't waste more time asking that. 'So, you're sure of the spelling.'

'I just told you that!'

He hadn't, of course.

'Ferente's her name. But she was married to a guy named Rousseau.'

'Does she go by Rousseau?'

'She could.'

How had this man lived this long without someone strangling him? 'R-o-u two s's e-a-u?'

'Like it sounds.'

'Wally, do you expect me to find her under this name?'

'You could.'

'Then why not cut to the chase and give me her phone number. Which . . . you . . . have?' *Dammit!*

The silence from his end went on so long I was on the verge of hanging up and calling again, when he said, 'Five one oh . . .'

East Bay.

I copied the rest of the number, repeated it – laboriously – thanked him and just about hung up.

'Don't tell her I gave it to you.'

'I won't.' I'll add your secret to Gracie's and Gary's.

'Tell me what she says.' There was such an earnestness to his request that I censored my first choice of response and just agreed.

I called her. Left a message and my numbers, changed into running clothes to whip by Gary's office and pick up the Aston Martin and make my way back here from wherever I could find a piece of curb in Gary's parking district to leave the car. If I veered back across Broadway here, I'd have to move that sedan every two hours. One scratch would cost more than I'd earned this calendar year.

The landline was blinking. A message.

'Hey, Darce' – it was Mike – 'here's the number . . . Two something . . . Wait.' The swish of fumbling mixed with a metallic buzz. 'Here. 287-4398. Wait . . . Sun's hitting the screen. Yeah, here, 237-4898. OK?' More phone rumbling. 'Be careful. You know that, right? Seriously. I should never have let you shove me on to the ferry. I almost jumped into the bay and swam back. I would have. You were watching me, right? Hey, sorry I missed you. And, well, thanks. I'll call later.'

I was so relieved I slid down to sitting and leaned against the wall, still holding the receiver.

Then I was annoyed.

I listened to the message again. What jumped out were his pauses. Mike was not a pauser. When I was a kid I assumed he possessed all knowledge. Later, I had the sense that his poise came from having chosen his role before a scene began. It gave me a queasy feeling and I'd always assured myself that while my favorite brother might cop a pose for others, he was natural with me.

Whatever the backdrop, Mike never hesitated, doubled back, allowed himself to sound exhausted . . . unsure – and, oh God, wary – like this.

Wary . . . and he didn't even know about the figure in the shadows or the cracking of his windshield. Or Gracie's steps. Or Gary's garage.

Damn it, if I had him on the line I could ask.

And Mike would say . . .?

I replayed the message, hoping I'd missed some positive allusion, or at least some better rationale for his uneasiness than the sun shining on the cell-phone screen. But, in fact, what I heard this time was worse. He'd misread the phone number he'd left me, one time or the other. Or maybe both.

I dialed first one, then the other. Neither did he answer. On neither had he remembered – or maybe bothered – to set up the message option. I'd missed him by half an hour! And unless I stationed myself here by the zendo phone, I'd probably miss him the rest of the day. Dammit. He had the answers. Adrienne Ferente, formerly Rousseau, who was she? Where was she? How did he end up house-sitting for her? Free gig? Free love? I dialed his number again. It rang and rang. Didn't even go to message. Just kept ringing.

If it even was the right number.

*When all things are dead ends, do the next thing.*

I called John.

As the phone rang I remembered his call two days ago. 'Call me,' he'd insisted. I had not.

That wasn't going to make this conversation better.

The call went to message.

The message said, 'I will be unavailable for the rest of the week. Leave a message if you want, but I won't be checking till the weekend.'

*When all things are dead ends, and the next thing is a dead end, then what?*

# TWELVE

Upstairs I found Leo moving his robes from the closet rack to a hook on the door, hand-brushing them, inspecting the edges for fraying. *The bell rings into silence*, he'd said, more than once, meaning that at zazen, the timekeeper does not ring the bell at the moment the period is scheduled to begin, but waits until latecomers have entered, settled on their cushions, and the room is silent. So that the bell is not just one more noise in the room, but a note once struck that pulls everyone into the communion of silence.

For Leo, the ritual of moving robes, getting dressed, walking downstairs and into the zendo was his preparation for the bell.

It meant I had time to change, too. But not to do anything else. Not that I had a plan, other than to go back to Mike's apartment and hope.

Leo glanced over as I reached the hallway. 'Take-out after zazen?'

'Sure.'

'Tacos?'

'Sure.'

He must have seen something in my face. He said, 'I'll make the call.'

'Thanks.'

When the bell rang into the early evening silence twenty minutes later, I let myself be pulled in by the widening ripples of the ever-softer reverberations. The candles that had been almost invisible when we entered flickered against dusk by the end. Sometimes zazen is a long flow of calm, sometimes it's thoughts yanking on the hem of your mind. You let one go, only to have it replaced by another. Some of both happened, but one thought kept pulling at me: burritos.

'There was this great burrito shop Mike took me to when I was a kid,' I said to Leo upstairs after zazen. 'Fish burritos before anyplace else had them. They actually put abalone in them. No one does that! God, it was good. I'd forgotten about it. Place with a funny name. Jansen's Burritos. I wonder if it's still in business. It'd be pretty far for take-out.'

He pulled out his phone, checked. 'Maybe they're there but no listing. Jalisco OK? I'll call and go get it.'

I did the phone check dance. Nothing from Adrienne – if, in fact, she'd ever gotten a message from Wally to call me. Nothing from Mike, not on the landline or my cell. 'I'm here till at least eight. Call me on the landline,' I said to each of their messages. 'Don't put it off. I'll just keep bugging you,' I added to Mike.

'Dinner!' Leo sang out twenty minutes later, as his rubber-soled shoes splatted on the stairs.

We Lotts have an erratic relationship with food. To a one, we're irresponsible about mealtimes. But when food materializes it's like a visit from an old and dear friend. We settle in for the duration. Or just about make pests of ourselves coming back again and again. Like with Jansen's chorizo and petrale burritos with the bits of abalone.

'Jansen's burritos?' Leo asked after we'd finished Jalisco's trout and guacamole. He was sitting cross-legged on his futon in his room, leaning back against the wall like a man making room for his stomach. The containers formed a centerpiece between us on the floor that passed for a table.

'Jansen married well. Mike said all the guy contributed to the restaurant was his name.'

Leo looked like he might have commented but didn't.

I was picturing Jansen's back then. 'The place was tiny – half a storefront wide; more like a food cart without wheels. The family'd had a restaurant in Mexico, I think. No one's English was more than passable. The youngest girl translated. But it didn't matter. The whole family knew Mike and made a big deal over me, his sister. They let me pretend I was employed in the burrito-making line. They were always refining my technique.'

He raised an eyebrow and reached for a bit of tortilla to scoop up the remains of the rice and salsa.

'Burrito building – not too much rice on the tortilla or it dulls down the taste of the fish. But too little and the juice squirts out as soon as the customer takes a bite. Know your Anglos who think they can handle chili and can't. Senora Perez had a watered-down bottle of hot sauce for them.

'Their burrito was huge. By the time they added the extra fish, extra beans, sour cream, it looked like a ham hock in a tortilla. Mike and I had to take two buses to stop there.' I was twelve, Mike sixteen. In three years he would disappear. 'Back then we'd go to a Giants game every month or so. Fans, but not big fans. We'd make a day of it: Jansen's for lunch, and then Candlestick, where you can freeze on any summer day. Mike's rule was keep eating to ward off the cold.' I grinned.

'I told Gary about all this after Mike disappeared. His assumption was Mike didn't care about the food, that he was meeting a girl there.'

'Was he?'

'John said, *What?*'

'Was he meeting a girl?' Leo had stopped eating and sat, just waiting.

He was asking not about the girl, but – I realized – about me. Had I noticed what Mike was doing?

'I don't think so. Girls flocked to him. He didn't have to go all that way. I'm sure . . .'

Leo caught my eye.

'OK, I *assume* there's no reason he would have. The whole food and ballgame was a ritual between us.'

*'To carry yourself forward and experience the myriad of thing . . .'*

It was a moment before I finished Dogen-zenji's teaching, *'. . . is delusion.'*

Eihei Dogen, the founder of the Soto school of Zen Buddhism was talking about enlightenment and delusion. But Leo wasn't.

'You mean me and Mike?'

He continued eating, leaving me to contemplate just what he did mean.

I returned to my dinner too. Nothing puts a Lott off her food. I could have pondered Leo's comment. Instead I tried to picture Jansen's, tried to see not the men cooking, not the mother folding napkins, the three daughters working the food line and the register, too busy to have time for Mike, not even the line outside blocking the driveway, the house next door and into its driveway, but to draw back the memory of the people nearby. While I was scooping white fish and chorizo with the slotted spoon, was Mike outside chatting up a girl? Dark hair? Blonde? A redhead like the two of us?

Could that have been the point of these trips?

Could the girl have been Adrienne Ferente? Was that the connection? Or was this a wild, desperate grab for illusion?

Adrienne Ferente whom, in any case, I couldn't track down.

Adrienne Ferente to whose apartment I had the key.

At 10.30 p.m. I scored a parking spot a block from Adrienne/Mike's apartment, on the street that borders the park panhandle, a wide grassy island between fast streets to and from the freeway. Haight Street might still have been popping, but Oak Street was as quiet as its rustic name indicated. Cars swished by on their way to downtown, or 101 north to the Bay Bridge or south to San Jose, but they were merely a river flowing beyond the shore. The Victorian houses that danced in blues and purples in daylight were shadowy frames for dim glows of computers or TVs. Occasionally traces of marijuana glided lazily across the sidewalk, as if it knew its days of being an illegal and thrilling danger were over and it was all but legal already. As if those fetors carried off bits of the Haight-Ashbury as they drifted over the rest of the city.

As the stampede of gentrification raced back over it.

I spotted Mike's house by Wally's open second-story window and the bright ceiling light. And the grumble and jolts of men's voices. The shades were up and Subhuti, the big guy from Jersey with the oddly Buddhist name, kept bouncing out of his chair.

The front door was locked, but I still had Mike's key. His apartment, on the ground floor, was dark. Good. I needed undisturbed time to uncover an address, a phone number, something to lead me to Adrienne's temporary place in the East Bay. And then there was the Glock in the bedroom drawer. Still there?

Before I could reach for the knob, a thump from above shook the hallway floor.

I headed upstairs. 'Hi,' I said, opening the unlocked door. The place looked like grad students had been in residence for a semester. Like a hurricane, a tornado and a flood had converged.

Like surfaces other than the floor did not exist. Like dishes of what must once have been food were dissolving into the jumble of blankets and clothes and books on the floor. 'Wow.'

Heather laughed. Tom looked sheepish. Subhuti – *Boots*, I recalled – glanced over at the source of the sound – me – and turned back to the computer screen.

'Good point, Tom, if nothing gets in your way,' he said, gliding over the slight disturbance of my arrival. 'Like Maroski said this morning, you got, what, maybe a year to make it.'

'But if your app's got legs—'

Boots brushed her off. 'Got legs? It walks. Away from you. You're lucky you get bought out. Not so hot, you fail.'

'But local—'

'Heather, my dear, they're all local. Look, like Jeffers said, you start a local service, you know, like valet for a day. Client places the order at midnight, for six a.m. Order goes to your hub here or maybe you've outsourced to Mumbai for overnight. Either way, it shoots back to humans. Either you got a guy in Ess Eff who texts local providers, or you've got that automated. But, bottom line, honey, the guy who presses the suit lives here.'

Heather rolled her eyes. Tom, his arm still around her shoulder, gave it a quick squeeze.

'Let's say you succeed, despite dealing with independent providers who are independent because they like working their own schedule. Despite customers making repeat deals directly with them and cutting out the middle man—'

'You?'

'Right.'

'Stuff happens,' Tom muttered in a way that suggested it had happened to him.

'Right. Provider gets a flat tire.'

'Or a better offer.'

'Can't find the address. Can't stand the client. Can't—'

'Got it,' Tom cut in.

'So you're big stuff. With luck you get a big buy-out.'

'Like you told me.' How many times?

'More likely you get shafted.'

'Like you told—'

'My point, Tom, is that you gotta work your ass off in that

year, 'cause that's all you're going to get. You gotta see it as a stepping stone. You gotta position yourself for the leap.'

Tom sighed, stood and said, 'Like you said.' And headed to the bathroom.

'Like yours.' Boots shifted to face Heather. 'You got your cold case, you got your crowd-sourcing. It's all local. Maybe you're in, say, Orono, Maine, but every bit of information you collected comes from someone local to the case, right?'

'Yes, but I sift it, post it to anyone, anywhere. I've been doing it for years and I know—'

He lifted a hand, effectively brushing off her observation on her own project. 'You don't got local, you don't got nothin'.'

Now I realized why the window was open. The slight aroma of marijuana didn't begin to cover the smell of going-bad food.

'Yeah, wow!' Wally, the curmudgeon in residence, peered out of the kitchen. He glared at our living-room trio, down at the wet bowl in his hands, and over at me, his expression of weary disgust never altering. It was like he clothed himself in long-suffering and the garb suited him. His face drooped into culverts, from his sunken cheeks to the troughs from the corners of his tight and downturned mouth. Does there come a time, I wondered, when a smile is no longer physiologically possible?

'You gave me the wrong number for Adrienne.'

'How—'

'She hasn't called back.'

From his expression, I might have said 'the sun's not rising at midnight,' or 'the impound lot isn't providing valet service,' or 'the threesome in the living room aren't planning a trip to the art museum.' But his gaze flickered to a drawer and back. 'I can check her number.'

'Just call her. Now.'

'It's the middle of the night! If it weren't for these clowns I'd be tucked in bed.'

'With her?'

'She wishes!'

It's said that men do not see their bodies as critically as do women. Even so, it was hard to imagine Wally standing in front of the mirror muttering, 'Come and get it, ladies.'

'Just call her. Tell her I'm driving you crazy and it's her fault.'

For once Wally stood silent. Apparently I had taken the words out of his mouth.

I started through the living room and said over my shoulder, 'I'm going downstairs to check something for Mike.'

Heather perked up. I had the feeling that she figured whatever I might do down there had to be more interesting than the argument up here. But before she could move, Tom, staring at the screen, wrapped his arm tighter around her shoulder. Boots reached into a big plastic bowl and pawed up a mound of orange cracker-y stuff. But not fast enough to cover a spark of jealousy.

Recalling the gun in Adrienne's bedroom downstairs, I glanced out the window. 'Hey, you guys, have you had any problems, danger-wise?'

Tom and Boot shrugged, but it was Heather I watched. She hesitated.

'Heather?'

She shook her head.

I held my gaze.

'Well, you know, I'm not from here, so maybe I'm just not ready for the city, you know?'

'But . . .?'

'Well, a couple times I had the feeling someone was following me. But then I looked around and there were just other people behind. No one—'

'Big, bad and scary,' Boots put in.

'Yeah,' Heather said, seeming relieved.

'I'll take you downstairs.' This from Wally.

'I'm fine.'

'S'OK. I'm going. Not hanging around here,' he said, eyeing the three, who were ignoring him.

I'd counted on being alone. But 'things as it is,' Suzuki-roshi said, intentionally ungrammatically. We suffer because we want things to be different than they are. So, I'd suffer Wally.

'What did the apartment look like before it was tossed? When Mike was just living there?' I asked as we headed downstairs.

'Like Adrienne had it.'

'Tidy?'

'Coulda been worse.'

Considering the room we just left, that comparison meant nothing. As he unlocked Adrienne's door, I said, 'Wally, is it dangerous here?'

'Danger's what you make it.'

'Hey, it's too late for philosophy.'

He looked at me, laughed, and shut the door behind us. Feet clattered down the steps, the front door opened and banged shut. Wally shrugged, as if one of his renters leaving in the middle of the night underlined his point.

I put a hand on his arm. 'Seriously. There was a gun in her lingerie drawer.'

I thought he'd be grabbing at me for details. What kind of gun? What kind of bra? Cotton? Lace? Titless?

But suddenly he was all landlord. 'A gun! I don't allow weapons on the premises. He knows that. Why'd he do a dumb thing like that?'

*He?* 'What makes you think it's his?'

'You mean *she* had it? Here? In this house for months?'

'I mean, I don't know. But you assumed Mike brought it. Why?'

Wally slunk back half a step, shoulders arching forward as if to protect his assumption. As if I was about to snatch a fact out of his gut. 'It's something he'd do.'

*I don't think so! Mike's never had a gun!* I froze, desperate to hide any reaction that could give Wally a clue and allow him to lead me down a path away from what he was protecting. I waited, letting the silence unnerve him.

Finally he said, 'People have a bad view of the neighborhood. Outsiders. But you live here, you know how it is.'

'Which is?'

'A neighborhood.' He stood a moment before pushing open the door. 'Adrienne's lived in this apartment for years. Now, all of a sudden, she needs firepower? She didn't mention it to me and, let me tell you, when there's anything she imagines in her strangest dreams to be wrong with this place, she's on the horn to me. She was carrying on about the people across the street – they're making a racket, she said. Saturday night yet! Music playing. What does she expect me to do about it? She knows the cops'll figure they're working overtime just to take down the address.'

'Still . . .' I said, hoping to squeeze a drop of illogic from his sensible reply. 'So why would Mike offer her the gun?'

'Maybe he didn't.'

'Let's say.'

'OK, maybe he wanted to get it here without carrying it himself.'

'It's not like you do pat-downs at the door here.'

'Listen, no guns—'

'Guns?' Heather was halfway in the door. She jumped back, smacking into Boots.

'No guns! Jeez!'

'Sorry. I can't be around guns since my parents were killed. I just . . . I can't.' She was still standing in the doorway leaning against Boots. He snapped his arms around her shoulders like he'd been offered a prize.

'Tom,' Boots said in the awkwardness, 'just got a big deal call and split.'

Ah, the stair clatter and door banging. 'At this hour?' I said.

He shook his head in condescension, and gave Heather's shoulder a squeeze. 'What kind of gun?'

'Glock. Nine millimeter.'

'Reliable.'

'You know guns, Boots?'

'Some. After my parents were killed—'

'Your parents died, too?' I said, amazed, then added, 'I'm sorry.'

'Not a big deal.'

*Really?*

'That always throws people when I say that. But they were guru groupies. They'd be off to India so much, to this great master or that one, that in the end it was like they just stayed at one of the ashrams, you know. They always stored me at my aunt and uncle's. So, you know, nothing changed for me. My parents, the last time they were home, it was like they were visitors. Wackos in Indian cotton in December. Complained about everything. America was awful, but in India it was all wonderful, not materialistic like Jersey.' His voice had been speeding up, his round pale face pinking. And his hand, I noted, had tightened on Heather's shoulder.

'I was better off with my uncle. We shot at beer cans in the backyard. I could hit the B at thirty feet. It gave me this great idea for an app.' He glanced behind him, as if competitors might have materialized just inside the door. 'I'm from Jersey. Roads are jammed there. Drivers go at it with one hand on the horn and the other on the top of the wheel so they're ready to flip the bird. So, I'm thinking, what about an app, dash mounted, pulling in video of the cars ahead, and a big-bang gun to take them out?' He grinned, then sent a wary glance behind him again and ended up looking sheepish.

Heather had been shrinking away from him and now shook free. He looked over at his arm hanging in air and seemed surprised. And let down.

Even Wally was edging back toward the door. 'Nerds!' he mumbled.

I didn't know what to feel. I walked to the window, pulled it open to let in the night air.

Which was how I came to see a dark figure standing back up as if he'd just checked under Mike's car. Or put something there. He started to walk toward Haight.

The streetlights were bright enough. It was the same guy who had been eyeing the car yesterday. I recognized him by his walk.

I grabbed my pack and raced out.

# THIRTEEN

I should have checked the car.

I'd worry about that later.

Famous last words.

But the guy, the one who I had spotted hanging around the car before (I recognized his stance, the way he moved; stunt doubles notice that kind of thing), was already at the end of the street, turning the corner on Haight. In a minute – less! – he could be squatting against the wall, head drooped, just another addict. Or in a bar. Or yuppie-ing his way down the aisle at Whole Foods.

I raced up the street after him, caught the edge of the corner building and swung myself onto Haight. Stopped dead. Went fuzz-focus, blurring people into background, eyeing the scene only for movement. Colors melted into each other, shadowy, dark. Auto lights became streams of white and red. Traffic lights eased back against the dark of the park in the distance. Wind whipped in from the sea, pricking my neck, my face, its vaguely briny smell cutting the stench of sidewalks never scrubbed, coats and blankets that never could be washed. A tree branch shimmied, snapped leaves down and up. Cars braked, engines roared up and eased into a slurry of city-noise. And then, like cherries and blueberries tossed into a blender, they meshed and I watched, waiting for one fleck, one movement, one man who couldn't be still long to brace or jerk. To reveal himself.

Low on the wall, a shifting lump. A man easing closer to a dark pile.

The pile moved.

A dog.

Across the street by the McDonald's, standing bright, bouncy-house-ish behind its apron of green grass, its short metal picket fence . . . Could my guy have gotten that far before I made it to Haight? Don't think. Just look. Something flowed around the corner of the edge of the fence into darkness.

The light at Haight and Stanyan turned green. Engines growled. I shot across the street in front, expecting horns and shouts, but none came, as if no one expected denizens to bother with crosswalks here.

The sidewalk was cluttered with people going nowhere, as if they were dark wads of crumpled paper. This last block of Haight, by Golden Gate Park, was like a visit to 1970. Nineteen seventy, with its mirrored dresses rusted and grayed, peacock feathers fallen to dust. No one moved. Even the golden arches seemed tarnished.

Inside McDonald's, people perched on the plastic 'don't sit here forever' chairs by the window tables were looking down. For them the dark night curtained the glass. The side door had been locked at nine and now, in less than half an hour, at eleven, the Haight Street door would close. Which meant customers had twenty minutes to snag a burger or, more vitally for many, wait in the slow and desperate line for the bathroom.

Across the street, in the park, sat the police station. You'd think . . . You'd be wrong. Reports of drug sales continue. Buyers slumped nearby as if waiting to be evidence.

I rounded the fence onto Stanyan. The scene, the year, changed. Ahead were Victorians, four-plexes, city housing in a neighborhood on its way up fast. Streetlighted, dim. A tall, thin man, tall plump woman, walking easily, his arm across her shoulder, her hand in his back pocket. To my right now, on the far side of the street, the park loomed dark. A thousand acres of places to hide. Cars waited, headlights quivering, their light not making it across Stanyan to my sidewalk.

Suddenly nothing was moving. Had I lost him? So soon? I wanted to run all out, to catch up. But which way in the unmoving darkness?

The McDonald's? Had he laundered himself from a culprit into a customer? I'd seen him only in shadows; would I recognize him in color? I took one stride toward the entrance and caught myself. Better to wait.

I hate to wait.

Breathe, Garson-roshi's told me. More than once. You think nothing's happened, but there's a world within your exhalation, a world you don't even know is there. Breathe.

I breathed. I kept my eyes on the franchise door and breathed.

Running is single-focused – move! Fast! Faster! Focus! Block out the inessential. Standing is unfocused, letting the inessential boil off. Brakes grinding. Tires squealing. Paper clattering in the wind. The wind, cold on my neck, my sweaty shoulders. Bile in the back of my mouth. Murky smell of muddy garbage. Dog nails on the sidewalk. Man in dreads slumped against the fence, wriggling to find comfort against the iron rods. Body lumped under sleeping bag, snoring, dog shifting to get more bag room. My breath coming fast. Not so fast. Perfume behind me. Pot. Sweat all around. Sweat steaming up from my armpits.

The door opening.

I leapt back against the wall.

'Watch it, broad!'

'Sorry,' I muttered, eyes on the man coming out of the store door. Carrying a four-burger brown bag. Was he going to run with that? Was he the same guy? *Don't assume.* I'd assumed all over the place about him. Was he even my guy? His walk, was it the same? His stance?

'Hey, broad, outa my space!'

The guy with the bag turned halfway – not far enough. But my cover was blown. I started toward him. 'Hey!'

He stopped. My height, shaved head, pale brown skin, round glasses. 'What?'

'Sorry, I thought you were someone else.'

'I could be.' He grinned.

Behind us cloth rustled, rubber soles hit pavement.

'Another time. Gotta go!' I whirled around in time to see a figure – the right guy – racing across Stanyan and into the park.

I started into Stanyan, but he – tall, lanky, loose – had whipped across before the light changed. Me? No way. Stepping into traffic now would be suicide. I waited, forcing myself to go into blur mode again. But the park's all blur, or near to it. All he needed to do was lie down under a bush or in among trees and I'd never find him.

And yet, he was after something. He'd been there the first night, hovering by the car outside Mike's apartment. Later, when I'd parked by the old Kezar Stadium, he'd tailed me back there. Same man? Probably. How many times had I spotted him near the car? Haunting the car.

Or haunting me?

Bottom line! After all that, he wasn't going to give up or go away.

Now, here, he was in the dark. I was under the streetlight.

His move.

The light changed. I could have crossed. I didn't. It changed back.

Eleven o'clock passed. I could tell by the sharp pronouncements of closing hour, the loud grumble of complaints from McDonald's. The light changed and changed back. The sidewalk filled, as if a huge ball of grumble had rolled on to it. I was tempted to move. Instead I stood still, allowed myself to be jostled by bodies that could have been more stable, could have smelled fresher. I wondered how long—

Something slammed me hard. I grappled for balance. A hand grabbed my jean's pocket. The guy was big, broad, long matted blond hair. He grabbed me around the waist, pulled me toward him, digging for my wallet.

I could have poked his eye. My hands were free, I could have sliced the side of his neck, pushed him off, caught him behind the calf and pushed him to the ground. I could have handled him. But I didn't.

Not till I heard brakes squeal, feet slap fast coming toward me. My target, abandoning his cover and running back toward me. I was reeling him in. I could have grinned.

Instead, I braced my teeth, banged my head back into the mugger's jaw, and lit out after my target.

# FOURTEEN

I checked the light, shot across Haight – not the direction I wanted – and tried to blend in before the light changed again and I could shoot across Stanyan.

Of course my target was not in sight. I'd have expected no less. He wasn't going to be cooling his heels right outside Park Station.

There was a flurry of nervous indecision around the police station from those hoping for the apron of its protection and those wanting to make tracks pronto. But move on a few yards into the park and you're in the dark.

My target could be needle-in-haystack-ing here in Golden Gate Park. It's a thousand acres of grass and shrubs, trees so tall and old they're in danger of falling over. It has a lake with an island, a conservatory, art museum, aquarium, two windmills and a herd of bison. It's like a whole city of hiding places intermingled with spots to leap off and pounce on lone women. Was I hanging on to the end of an invisible leash, trailing him, as I assumed, or could the collar be around my neck?

Or was it the other way around? Did he just assume he was luring me? That the collar was not around his own neck? Which one of us had the business end of the leash? I'd been to the park plenty as a kid. Been to Kezar Stadium long after the 49ers moved to Candlestick, way long before they moved to the suburbs of another city. I'd run in high-school track meets in Kezar, then loped across the park and home. Mike and I'd found our dog here after she'd been lost three days.

I walked on past the police station. The smell of pine mixed with the suddenly stronger brine from the wind off the ocean. Suddenly colder. It rustled my jacket, snapped my hair against my face.

'Wanna party, Red?' The man came out of nowhere. It was that kind of area. Tall. In clothes that fit him forty pounds ago. Light brown hair that might have started as dreads but were now just matted. Coat suitable to Nome.

I shook my head.

'Buy a bag?'

*Right, like I'm going to buy an illegal substance in the cop's backyard.* 'Not now.'

He shrugged and shifted away. I caught his arm. 'Hang on. I'm hunting a tall, lanky white guy. He just ran in here from across Stanyan? You see him?'

'Nah.'

My target could have trotted over his stomach and this guy wouldn't have noticed. I still had him by the arm, a thick wad of hardened wool around a stick of an arm. How old was he? It's hard to tell with the wasted. Forty? Thirty hard years? Life a stretch of laconic desperation, interspersed with sudden bad decisions and not much to lose?

And I was trotting into the dark empty park with him! 'Walk with me, OK?'

'Sure. Yeah.' He brightened. 'You reconsidering?'

'You certain you didn't see him?'

He glanced around, checking for cops? For buddies? Competitors? But the area was still as a painting. It looked empty. Empty enough that he eyed my backpack.

'Don't even think about it!'

'I was just—'

'Don't! You saw something; help me and I'll pay. Go for my pack and, trust me, you'll regret it.'

We were on the path by Kezar Road. I'd run along here last night, racing for the car. Then headlights were unnerving. Now they were white moments of safety. He didn't respond. The man was weighing his options. Was it worth it to assault me this close to the police station? On a traveled road? In sight of park regulars who might rescue me and turn him in? Or who might hyena me, the lot of them.

'Fifty.'

I forced a laugh.

'Forty.'

'Twenty-five and you put his hand in mine.'

'Thir—'

I stopped under a streetlight. 'Twenty-five and that's it.'

'No point in getting out of bed for twenty-five!'

I just stared.

'OK, OK. Over there. Across the road.'

'Behind the bushes?'

'Hey, Sugar, it's all behind them.' He shook off my hand, shifted, reached for my arm. I let him take it. Let him lead me across the road, him holding up a hand like a crossing guard. Cars barely slowing.

His hand slipped on to my shoulder.

I let it stay. 'Point the way.'

'Straight ahead. Like I said, behind that bush, the one with the flowers.'

'Point.'

'Huh?'

'Just fucking do it!'

'Jeez, you don't have to get all foul-mouthed!'

I almost laughed. 'Would you please point?'

He pointed to the bush with the flowers. White flowers, like the bushes in the freeway dividers.

The bush didn't move.

But twenty feet to the right, the limb of a low tree shifted in wind that wasn't blowing that way.

I took off running.

'Hey, Sugar, my twenty!'

'Later.' I dove through the branches, breast-stroking them out of my way. Cut sharp left, then right along the path someone else wouldn't see. Wind whipped the branches; fog-shrouded moonlight flashed and was gone.

Suddenly I was furious. I yelled, 'I hate being used!'

A downed log blocked the way. I leapt it. 'You're going to pay!' My shoe landed in mud.

'You led me through mud! You miserable untrustworthy piece of scum.'

I stopped. But I wasn't blur-looking now. Wasn't listening for a telltale sound. I was shaking.

There was no point in going on any farther.

I wanted to scream as loud as my voice would carry, 'I hate you!' But pride kept me silent.

Instead I said, not loud, just regular, 'I don't even know you.'

# FIFTEEN

Every emotion I had swirled through my body, as if a cook was pouring every bottle in the kitchen into a blender. I'd felt like this only twice before. When I admitted to my husband – my soon-to-be ex-husband – that my brother Mike had been missing so long that all logic said he was dead. When I stood at the edge of a forty-foot drop on to a catcher bag I wasn't sure would hold. Wind hit me in gusts. I couldn't gauge how far it could blow me off mark. In that moment – 30 seconds to go or give up – fears took on colors. Broken back – Army green. Broken neck – mud brown. Quitter – lumpy yellow. Scorn – maroon. Losing my chance to be a stuntwoman ever again – black. Death – clear. They swam in a sweaty circle, bubbled, lumps swashing lumps, colors mixing in an indistinguishable murk until I couldn't tell one from the other, could remember what they were, couldn't think. The swirl took me over, blotted me out. Only it existed.

And then, for one short instant, I hooked my eyes on the mark on the catcher bag, felt the wind ease. And I jumped.

Now, in the near dark, under the heavy evergreen branches, I focused on the spot between my brother's eyes and I jumped.

More accurately, I said nothing. No lead. No open path to diversion. I waited for him to tell me the truth.

His version of it.

He waited, watching me like a dog does to note your initial shift so he can run ahead and pretend he's not following you.

*You incredible louse!* I was shaking so hard I had to jam my teeth together so they wouldn't clatter. *You are the stalker. You!*

My body was steaming, my skin freezing, my heart pounding like a sledgehammer. I wanted to hit him for getting into this, to hug him for being OK. Oddly, the thing I felt most was an understanding of Boots's reaction to his self-absorbed parents.

I waited.

'I'm sorry,' Mike said. He sounded sorry.

I've heard his impressive 'sorrys' – to Dad, to John, to cops when he was doing fifty in a twenty-five zone. He never got a ticket.

I snorted.

'No, really.'

'So what? You've run me around for two days like a kid's battery car. If I'd gotten to your place half an hour later I could have been blown up. Did you think of that?'

'Sorry.'

'Forget sorry. What the hell is going on?'

The man who'd hunched over the car, the guy in the bulbous down jacket, stretched out of that cocoon into Mike. I'd seen him in disguise before. He'd fooled me before. It's not just the clothes or a wig, he'd said, it's the way you move, the way you stand when you're not moving. People see what they expect to see. They fill in the gaps. More to the point, they don't see what they don't expect. And if they're about to see, you just need to divert them. He was, no doubt, right, but he hadn't adjusted for me, a sister who had spent years watching him, a stunt double who'd spent years analyzing moves, a stunt coordinator who'd spent weeks watching every minute shift her stunt doubles made. Mike could have fooled the entire rest of humanity, but not me.

He was dressed like a street person. He yanked out a filthy handkerchief and gave an enormous snort into it. An empty snort but, in my mind, even after what he'd just told me, that handkerchief was filled with vile germy green goo.

He unzipped the down jacket, revealing a gray cotton sweater. With the knit cap off, his curly mahogany hair bounced in the wind, seeming to catch light that wasn't here. He reached around my shoulder to pull me next to him, as he had so often in all the years I'd never questioned him. When we'd walked steps in sync like a regular and upsized version of the same being. People had stared. They'd smiled. We'd smiled back. Me because I was with the brother I trusted. He . . . I don't know why.

'I'm waiting, Mike.'

He pulled back his arm, the look on his face more pained and shocked than Boots's had been when Heather stepped out of his reach. Boots had merely lost a brief hope. Mike was seeing his skill at managing the world slip away. *Yeah, right, Mike! If you can't deceive the person who most wants to believe in you, what are you, huh?*

'Darce, you weren't in danger. I was watching you the whole time. When I got off the ferry I hitched a ride back to the city—'

'With?'

'A girl.'

'Who just happened to be heading across the Golden Gate?'

His shoulder scrunched in a little 'our-secret' shrug. 'Not exactly.'

'I'm not going down that path. Whatever you told her, fine. You being outside the apartment – fine! Chasing me from there to the car, that was you, too?'

'Well yeah. I wasn't going to let you wander through the park at night. If I'd realized how much better shape you're in than me . . . After you drove off I could barely stumble out of the park.'

'Yeah, well. You tailing me; that cancels out the last couple days for both of us. You could have just told me what was going on and saved me the hassle.'

He shifted away from me.

'Which you are going to do right now.'

He tapped his tongue on the roof of his mouth, thinking. And made a tiny clucking sound he mustn't have noticed. All the years he was missing, I could have found him in a crowded room just by that clucking sound. But I couldn't let myself think of the past. I was barely holding it together. I braced myself and waited.

'I'd tell you who was threatening me, why they were – if I knew. If I'd known I'd've dealt with it before this. Then, when I had to leave my own place, I would have stayed with Mom. If I'd had a solid lead, I'd've told John and let the cops deal. I'd never have involved you. But Darce, I don't know! Trust me.'

*I wish.* 'Tell me what you do know. Now!'

He nodded ahead and broke trail through the brush to a path near the Conservatory of Flowers – one we'd used when we were adolescents, when we wanted to talk, to plan. A 'need-to-know' path, safe from unwanted eyes. I followed, my eyes level with the back of his neck, as they had been in the last year before he disappeared. I could have walked beside him, the trail was just wide enough, but he wanted to break trail, I could tell. Because he didn't want me to catch him concocting his next 'truth.'

I caught his arm, ready to spin him to face me.

'What?'

'Nothing, Mike. I just tripped on something.'

He stiffened. He knew me, too. I'm steady on my feet. Or maybe it was my voice that gave me away.

*Things as it is.* What did I know? Not what he was thinking. Not what had occurred while he was missing all those years. Or before. Or even since he'd been back. He'd told me someone was threatening him now, but could I even be sure of that?

*Things as it is.* He had taken over the apartment under Wally. In the bedroom was a Glock. In his living-room drawer were a Giants ticket, a zipper pull, an abalone shell.

A small abalone shell. Too small to be taken legally.

The shell of an illegally harvested abalone. Why had he saved that?

There was a time I would have asked about the gun first and I would have believed his answer. Now I watched him without directly focusing and prepared to gauge his replies as I circled toward what he was hiding. 'Tell me about the abalone.'

'What?'

I didn't even start with the shell in his drawer. 'When you were diving, in high school?'

'I didn't dive. Not more than once.'

'Yeah, right. Those abalones just crawled into your trunk because they wanted to see the city?'

'Hey, it's dangerous up there beyond Fort Bragg. The water's rough. Waves shoot in, tides pull divers out too far from shore. And it's cold.'

'Still, a hundred dollars a pound?'

'Wasn't that much back then, but equivalent. You know what that means, little sister? Serious divers don't fool around. They're not risking their necks so they can share with novice kids from the city.'

I nodded. 'Guys die every year.'

'Novices. They go too deep, stay down too long. No oxygen – oxygen tanks are illegal. Fish and Game's all over the scene. Guys come for the day, rent gear; they don't want to go home empty. Water's roiling up sand and muck. It's not so easy to spot abalone down there, particularly if you don't know what you're doing. You trying to hold your breath long enough. Just one more crevice. Just a little deeper. Maybe your fin gets caught and you don't surface. Maybe you get swept out and when you do surface you're facing a cliff with no way up. Maybe you die.'

'Your point?'

'It's easier to buy from the guys who dive.'

'At a hundred dollars a pop, or equivalent?'

'Hardly.'

'From poachers,' I clarified.

He shrugged.

Red abalone is strictly protected. The limit is three per day. In a whole season you can take only eighteen in California, only nine in Sonoma County where Mike had been. They have to be nine inches or more. Guys, I'd read, dived with rulers. Abalone is a delicacy. A skilled poacher can make a thousand dollars in two days.

There was a time when Mike would have been furious at men decimating the stock. He—

My breath caught.

Wrong! There was a time when I believed he would have been furious.

I exhaled slowly. *Don't go down that path either.* 'So you knew the poachers. They knew you. Why would they sell to you when they had restaurants and the like waiting for them?'

'More like a tip. I kept watch; they tipped me in mollusk.'

'Why . . .?'

'Why'd I do it? I was sixteen. Alone on the cliff in the wind, with danger all around me. It was like being a movie hero. I'll tell you I had a few close calls. One time I was on the cliff and Tam, the guy I was watching for, signaled. His floater—'

'Floater?'

'It's like an inner tube with a slipcover.'

'Really?'

'Hey, you gotta keep your catch someplace. You can't use all your energy swimming to shore with each shell. Besides—'

'If he stashed them on shore someone would snatch them.' I was finishing his sentences. Like the old days. We were sailing in words, Mike and me. 'Some kid like you, right?'

'Well, yeah. Good car; great engine, and no one knew the back roads better than I did.' He was grinning.

I remembered that car, a gray Nissan, a pay-me-no-mind car. Mike used to ease up next to some other kid piloting a bright, haven't-had-its-first-scratch car. The kid would eye Mike with pity, or better yet, scorn, like he was driving his parents' car. Then Mike hit the gas and whipped by. Us two laughing.

It was the car I'd been in when he drove me past Ethan Kozlowski's house, me scrunched down, eyes just higher than the window bottom, squinting for a sighting of my heartthrob. Mike laughing at me, but still driving me.

So easy. So very tempting to slide back into these times, the memories that warmed my hopes after he disappeared. And now he was here and we were talking about them together. I loved it.

He knew I loved it.

I froze, focused on the tree ahead, a magnolia, on its salad plate leaves, waxed to a shine even at night. I breathed in slowly.

Under the magnolia, Mike's shoulders tightened.

Before he could chart the next detour I said, 'No one knew the back roads better than you. Why was that? All you needed was to get to the drop point, sit on the rocks and watch till there was no more light for diving. Then drive home, tired, maybe in the dark. Hungry, with food waiting to be cooked in the trunk. But you knew all the back roads. Why was that?'

I hadn't raised my voice but there was something different in my tone. I don't know whether I recognized that from the sound in my head or from Mike's reaction, the slightest jolt backwards, as if he was seeing someone else in his sister's skin.

As if we weren't us.

There are moments of pure balance when one tiny shift will drop you on either side. I was desperate to leap down the way I'd come, to step in the footprints that had fit my feet so long.

*Things as it is.*

I stayed still. Then I shifted to the side of reality and stepped down on to its cold, hard ground. 'Why was that, Mike?'

He made an odd move with his head that I had never noticed for itself before. But now, with nothing else to observe, I realized it was the precursor to my brother's deciding what character to play.

'Hey, the truth!'

'Darce—'

'Never mind. Let me tell you. There was a time, I remember, when you were still spending whole days in Fort Bragg but you weren't bringing home abalone any more. Mom waited for your abalone. A couple times she had everything ready when you arrived empty-handed.'

'She said she could as easily make something or other else.'

'She *said.* What was she going to do, stamp her feet and wail?'

'Hey, I called for take-out. She didn't have to do anything. And once we went out to dinner, all nine of us. On me!'

I nodded. It had been a great dinner. At a not-inexpensive Italian restaurant. Drifts of memory from that meal wafted through Mike-talk for years after he vanished. All of us Lotts there, everyone on decent behavior. Mom wearing a Navaho pendant Mike had given her for her birthday the week before. 'You had a lot of money for a high-school boy with no job. Suddenly.'

His head shifted again. Another time it would have amused me to see him oblivious to his *tell*. 'Don't bother whole-clothing about the money. Let me explain where you got it. You were still going to Fort Bragg, not dealing with the divers, because . . . because you'd found something more profitable. Less dangerous? Oh, OK, not less dangerous. Of course, because avoiding danger wasn't an issue.' I was reading him as I went. 'Dangerous in a different way. And it mattered that you knew the back roads. What could that be? You want me to go on guessing, or do you want to tell me the genesis of these last couple days of my life you've co-opted. Of what you insisted was a big threat?'

I thought I saw that neck movement. But it was just the wind fluttering leaves. He wasn't that bad.

'That coast up there, Mike, it's wild, rocky. No matter how many men Fish and Game had, they could never patrol the whole thing. They might as well build a wall like people want to do along the whole Mexican border.'

Now the neck movement.

'Oh! Easier to slip into the country from the ocean, right? If you're a big fish with money, right? Particularly if there's a smart kid like you on land keeping an eye out.'

I will say this for my brother, he knows when to fold. He

leaned against the magnolia and said, 'I learned the tides and the dirt roads. Once I hit the freeway, the old Nissan was next to invisible. I came equipped: portable wipe down, battery hair dryer, cologne that changed a man's odor from brine to musk. Change of clothes that meant change of nationality. American shoes. A fast boat drops an hombre before sunset. I get a "local" to San Fran in time for a late dinner.'

I asked, though I knew the answer. 'What kind of men?'

'Men who could afford to pay.'

'For the boat?'

'And me. When I learned what they were making, I figured why not me? I raised my price. They didn't haggle.'

We were silent a moment, then he said, 'Does this change how you think of me?'

'Well, yeah! But, do you mean, do I love you less? I don't know. Will I still help you now? Yeah.'

He seemed relieved. Like my trust in him really mattered to him.

'So,' I said, winding back to my withheld question, 'what's going on now? Who's threatening you? The truth.'

'I told you the truth.'

'Mike!'

'I told you the truth. Why would I lie when I needed your help? I never said I'd stay in Marin. Never said I wouldn't keep an eye on you and collaterally the danger to you . . . and me.'

'And you conclude?'

'Zip.'

I wanted to believe him. But who he was and how much I could trust this man was too big a knot to untangle now. 'Tell me this. Why did you give Adrienne Ferente your gun?'

He stopped, turned and faced me with an expression I hadn't seen since he'd been back. He looked stunned. 'I don't have a gun.'

'There was a Glock pistol in her lingerie drawer.'

'Just lying there in sight? Not in a box? Wrapped in a towel even?'

'Stuck business end in her bra.'

Mike was tapping his teeth, thinking. Not plotting – I knew that look. This one was fitting the pieces together.

'Like it had been put there in a hurry. Not tossed, but placed. A hurry but not a panic. Like,' I said, 'Adrienne's ride was honking. She realized she had it in her purse and didn't want to take it.'

'Lame.'

True. I made a come sign with my hand.

He shrugged.

'Hey, not good enough! Think. This is escalating fast. Gracie was sideswiped walking to her car—'

He stood frozen. He wasn't posing or concocting this time. He really was shocked, distressed, and then frightened. 'Is she . . . Is she all right?'

'She says she's OK, but she didn't go to work—' I waved off his attempted interruption. 'You know I've got Gary's Aston, right? You saw me go get it?'

'No. I've been watching my apartment, not everywhere you go.'

'Oil on Gary's garage floor. He kept his footing, but it could have been bad. My point—'

'I get your point!' He slumped down on a log and held his head.

I wanted to put my arms around him.

I didn't.

In a minute he stood. 'I was an idiot to let this happen, to think I could . . . It's over. Stay here. I'll get the car. Let's just get out of here and figure out our next move.' He felt in his pocket and then stuck out his hand. 'Give me the keys.'

I could have stopped him, but I needed a few minutes to clear my head, to deal with the swirl of emotion that threatened to suck me down. One look at him told me he needed the time, too.

We'd reached the end of the wooded area, close to the park panhandle bordered on its long sides by fast roads to and from the freeway.

'I'll watch my back,' he said, as if reading my mind.

# SIXTEEN

S*tay here, I'll get the car* meant, *Stay here, I'm going to do something I don't want you to see, to be involved in, or be endangered by.* I knew Mike.

I could have followed him and maybe escaped his notice, but it was a toss-up as to whether that would create more danger than what he planned. I assumed he was headed to check out the gun in the drawer of the apartment where he was, in theory, staying. I couldn't stop him. I could only impede him, or draw attention to him. With our dark red curly hair, Mike and I both get our share of stares, but when we're together we almost always draw attention.

So I waited, watched cars shoot out of the park, onto Oak Street. I checked messages. Zip. Two trucks ran the red light. A driver on Stanyan leaned on his horn and then shot through the intersection to make up for the three seconds lost.

Behind me leaves rustled. Branches rubbed and crackled. I turned in time to see a man emerge.

'Hey, what about my fifty?'

I laughed.

'Hey! No laughing matter, lady. Deal's a deal. You oughta know that.'

I nodded, but he wasn't ready to wind down. 'You gotta job, right? You work, you get your money. You know that.'

'You're right, you're right,' I repeated to stretch out my comment long enough to interrupt him. 'But it was twenty-five.' I pulled off my pack and dug for my wallet.

Two twenties. Nothing else.

'Hey, lady, I don't have all night.'

This side of sarcasm, there was nothing to say. I checked my watch. Fifteen minutes Mike had been gone. Five minutes max to the apartment. Another five if there was a problem – people in the hall, people in the apartment itself, something else. Two to check the gun. What's to see in a Glock? Five to get the car, make a square around the blocks – all right turns, no traffic light till this corner.

I said, 'Hang on a couple minutes. I'm waiting for a ride. I'll get a five from him.'

'You sure he'll come?'

'You saw us together, right?'

He shrugged. Translation: saw and eavesdropped.

A patrol car shot around the corner onto Oak Street, flashers ablaze.

The guy shrank back.

It cut right. Up Mike's street.

Just one car. Could be anything.

A second followed, Code Three. Its siren sliced the night noise.

Cops always call back-up.

The street guy swayed between the urge to disappear and my unpaid debt.

No way could I stand here and wait.

If Mike pulled up and I wasn't here, then what?

I said to the guy. 'I'll make you a deal. Forty bucks. You wait here for ten minutes. If an old white Honda with big black rubber bumpers slows down like the driver's looking for me, wave him over and tell him to call me. His sister.'

'If he doesn't show?'

'Ten minutes, that's all I'm asking.'

*I could be out of here in a minute. If you're gone how're you going to know?* he had to be thinking.

'If my brother comes and doesn't see you, I'll hear about it.'

'I wasn't—'

An EMT van switched on its sirens.

I held out the two twenties. 'Your name?'

I thought he'd fuss, but he pocketed the bills and said, 'Ventano.'

'Ventano?'

'Ventano Schwartz.'

'You got a phone?'

'Sure.'

'Give me your number? I'll call you.'

He hesitated.

'Ventano, this is business. If I were a cop you'd've been in cuffs the first time I spotted you.'

He gave. I keyed it in, let one more wave of cars flow after the light changed, hoping to see the Honda, but knowing it was futile. And then I shot across Stanyan, up Oak and on to Mike's block.

Patrol cars littered the street like toys abandoned at snack time. Flashers battled each other, turning the houses pinks and mauves, the street blood brown. Mike's white Honda shone red.

Across the street from Mike's window a woman leaned around her door. 'Was that a shot?'

'Sounded like it,' the man in the next house called back.

They might have been talking spinach prices. Or abalone. They stood, tableau-like, then shrugged as one and slipped back into their dwellings.

Gunshot! It was as if I'd already known. And yet I was desperate for it to be something else. A gas explosion, a fire. Something that had been set in motion while Mike was still in the park with me. That happened before he could have gotten here. Could have run into the house.

Could have scooped up the gun.

Could have come upon the person who would shoot the gun. Who would kill him.

'Gunshot. Gunshot.' A loose knot of people was forming, muttering, questioning, the flasher lights turning them into a ghostly chorus. A man spoke above the engine noises. 'Gunshot. No question about it. I stayed in a hotel in the tenderloin a couple nights when I first got here. Trust me, I know gunshots.'

I stopped, tried to listen the way I'd learned in the zendo. Bare awareness. Hear sounds, don't name them. Don't block anything out.

But I was naming like mad, looking for sounds to name, categorize, to give me explanations. Was that footsteps on stairs inside? Was that a voice? A cry? Upstairs? Downstairs in Mike's apartment?

Mike's windows were dark. Upstairs light shone through but not bright.

Two uniformed cops emerged from the walkway between houses. They mounted the outside stairs, banged on the door.

No answer.

'Police! Open the door!'

Nothing.

I dredged Mike's key out of my pocket and shoved it into the lock. 'Was it a gunshot?' I asked the cops.

'We'll find out.' The door swung open, slammed into the wall. I followed them in.

'Hey, lady, get back. You don't know what's up there.'

'I—'

'Out!'

*Up there!* Upstairs. Not Mike's apartment. I was so relieved I was embarrassed.

Not Mike. Mike was OK.

Hardly. He knew how to climb stairs.

I stumbled down to the sidewalk. In those couple minutes the crowd had doubled. An EMT van skidded around the corner. Back doors sprang open, spitting out paramedics, the light inside dazzling against the dark night. The intimate faux boudoir view almost obscene. Gurney out. Doors shut, paramedics racing to carry bed to the stairs.

I turned to two men behind me. 'Did you see anyone go in before? Anyone come out?'

'Nah. I was up on the street, heading home after a—' he glanced around at the police vehicles – 'an event. I figured why not stop and see what's happening, you know?'

'You?' I asked his companion.

He just shrugged.

I eyed the crowd, frantically looking for anyone familiar, anyone who'd been on the street when I got here. Red lights flashed on them erratically, each to its own beat, turning them into Photoshop images. No one looked real. None familiar.

A trio rounded the corner from Haight. Woman in long flowered skirt, spaghetti-strap top despite the damp cold of the night. Long frizzy mahogany hair. Phone in hand.

'Who're you got? What's he say?' A bearded guy with a rattail asked her.

'Skybo. Hold on a minute. Sky, like what's up here? Oh, you're here. Yeah, I see you.'

Tall, bone thin, and still wearing T-shirt and yoga pants

from fatter days, Skybo scarecrowed over to us. 'Code Three stuff.'

'And?' I prodded.

'Hey, who're you?'

One of the group eyed me. 'You've been here. What'd you see?'

'Cops. Medics. Headed to the upper unit.'

'Where those techies are.'

Omigod, Tom, Boots, Heather! Could it be—

'Airbnb!' someone behind them grumbled.

'What're they paying for a single fucking night?'

'More than you are for a week, sweetie.'

'Yeah, till my lease is up and my landlord can cash in, too.'

I swallowed, stared up at the suddenly over-bright second-floor windows, at the blue-uniformed bodies shifting at top speed.

Two more cars, a black and white, and an unmarked. Drivers abandoned the cars at angles, blocking the street. Squad leader and driver, a man in a suit. Detective. Their flashers were still turning the street from dark to fireplace red, mixing with the beat of the other official vehicles. Pause to black and repeat. Across the street, shades were drawn tight but doors were open. No one was sleeping through this.

Scenes like this reminded me of *Gone With the Wind*. Of Dante.

John, my cop-brother, used to grumble that the biggest threat to securing a scene was other officers rolling up to check it out, stepping over the crime-scene tape, planting their footprints over any residue of perpetrators'. Cops snarking to each other, overheard by witnesses who wouldn't even realize their perceptions had been colored before they could be interviewed. 'Tweeting, fer gawd's sake.'

I moved closer into the detective's path. I needed a quick make on him before he noticed me. I've crossed paths with SFPD often enough to have a reputation – good or bad, depending on the eyes of the beholder. This beholder wasn't familiar. So far, so good. What about Mike, who had had his own spotty past with the police before he disappeared, one I knew only by the tip of the iceberg?

Mike! I shot a look up at the second-story window. Was he there? He'd had plenty of time after he left me. After I'd told him about the gun.

Before witnesses heard it fire.

If he was up there . . . But I couldn't let myself think the worst. *Things as it is. Things as it is!*

I had to get in there and find out.

# SEVENTEEN

Was Mike in the house? Were the EMTs working on him?

Or worse, no longer working on him?

A woman in uniform strode out. Cops don't walk, they only stride. I could have asked her for an update, but it's a harder go with a woman. A guy will give a girl leeway, more if she's young and pretty. Try those moves with a woman and she'll snort in your face. Especially a woman in a macho job. Trust me. I've snorted at wannabe stunt doubles.

So I waited, listening to watchers speculate, flip those maybes and stroll down the other side, me staring up at the window for a glimpse of the victim, hoping against hope for sight of blond hair, brown, black, gray, anything but red. The idea that had started as a long shot was solidifying in my mind. *Don't assume!* But I'd assumed it into granite.

Were the cops going to let me in? Answer my questions? Not likely. But there was an outside staircase to Wally's apartment. He probably used it to take out the garbage. I could creep up, stand on the edge of the landing, peer in. If the back door had been left open, I could slip in.

The next cop out the door gets my question. No answer and it's around back and up.

Nothing had changed but I felt better.

A minute later a patrolman clomped down the front steps. Young, olive-complected, shaved bald, with a garlic bulb nose. Not a perfect choice. But I couldn't stand here in the street forever. 'Excuse me.'

'Yes?'

'The victim, is it Tom, the guy from Pennsylvania? He might not have any ID. And the conference—'

The cop – Santadomingo – pulled out a pad. 'Describe him.'

'Young, white, sandy hair, thin. Geek-pale.'

He started to shake his head and caught himself. 'Your name?'

Shit. The last thing I wanted was to be on record here. If Mike . . . whatever. My name – bad. 'Darcy. This is . . . uh.' I looked at the nearest man in the clutch of people behind me.

The man scowled at me, but said to the cop, 'Desmond Drayer.'

By the time the rest of them had given their names, I was desperate. But Santadomingo was between the door and me.

'She—' a woman named Chloe was pointing to me – 'saw a dude scoping out the place.'

'Go on, Ms . . . uh . . . Judd.'

Damn! She was going to land me in an interview booth at the station till dawn. Or worse she'd start talking about the lower apartment where Mike had stayed. Full of his fingerprints.

And the gun. Even if it wasn't his, had he picked it up?

How long would it take SFPD to run fingerprints?

If he wasn't lying dead in the apartment above.

Despite the wind, the cold, sweat coated my back. I checked the door again, then eyed the alleyway.

Santadomingo's walkie-talkie buzzed on his chest. He turned to shield it from us with his body and shifted his chin to it.

I moved behind him, whipped up the few stairs into the first-floor lobby. Mike's apartment was dark, but the lobby clattered like the inside of a drum. Feet in leather, feet in boots, voices calling over each other. Something – a gurney? – being pushed across the floor, banging something else. Outside a horn started to beep and kept beeping.

'No entry, miss,' the patrolman said.

'I'm ID-ing the victim.' I chin-pointed to the street. 'Santadomingo . . .'

'What?'

'Officer Santadomingo, right down there!' I sounded annoyed. Good. 'You want me to get him back here?'

He shrugged.

I took the stairs two at a time. All I needed was a second and a clear shot at the victim. To see his hair. Even just his hand, that hand I'd held as a kid. I pictured the patrol woman who'd strode out minutes ago, squared my shoulders, looked through her eyes as they teach in acting class. *Body language is half the battle.* In stunt doubling it's closer to ninety percent. I strode in.

The upstairs living room was train station full. Men talking into body mikes. Women measuring, noting. Everyone talking over everyone. The windows were open but there's no way to clear the smell of chemicals and death. I could have retched but Lotts don't upchuck. Involuntarily I squeezed my eyes shut against the smell, as if they would burn.

I snapped them open.

There was no victim.

He – or could it be she? – had to be in the bedroom.

In the doorway blocking entry to the bedroom was the last person I wanted to encounter.

Detective Higgins. Maybe I had once known her first name and blocked it out. Or more likely I'd ignored it to begin with. She'd been merely 'Officer' Higgins at our first encounter, and 'Officer' seemed more appropriate than Clarice or Dawn.

Higgins had reason to resent John, reason to despise me. She had been attached to a departmental clique under the protection of an inspector who was arrested for graft. By John. The guy nearly did time; only his connections saved him. His underlings just did more time in their ranks before promotion. But money had been lost, power lost, big-time expectations blown, and replaced by the bureaucratic equivalent of walking a beat. And no one in the department ever forgot. 'Higgins, who could have been . . .' 'Bare ass on the wrong horse.' Big laughs behind her back.

That thanks to John. Then there was me.

Higgins was about my age, near forty. White, not short but still squat, hair too blonde and cut in a place where people take their kids. Army tan jacket and slacks, spanning her overlarge butt. My opinion, of course, but I'd failed to hide it. And worse, I'd done so in front of a detective she had the hots for, who had the warms for me.

If she could have tossed me to the floor and stomped on my face, she would have. And no decent person would have blamed her.

Now she was huddled with a gray-haired man in a brown suit. Too old to be a cop; too soon to be from the medical examiner's office. But from her deferential stance, important.

Behind her, in the bedroom, a door slammed. A great wave of death smell washed up my nose. I gagged. Saw her gag.

I clamped my hand over my nose. As if that would make any difference. Then I shot past her, shoved aside the uniform at the bedroom door and pushed in.

'Hey, who the hell are you?'

'The scene!' *Don't let her compromise the scene.* 'Get her out of here!'

'You want me to identify the victim or not?'

Everything stopped. The cop in front of me moved aside. A tech squatting next to the body pushed himself up. Talk ceased. Time stopped, and the moment before I would see my brother lying on the floor or know he was OK stretched to infinity. Scenes from all the years he'd been missing scrolled before me: the deadened Thanksgiving dinners with us all sitting slightly farther apart because his chair was gone, the leads from detectives or research or luck coming up empty one after another, the gnawing ache none of us could ever bring ourselves to put into words lest that make it permanent.

I squeezed my eyes shut, took as much of a breath as I could tolerate and looked down at the body.

'Not him!' I said.

'Excuse me?' one of the cops said. 'Not who?'

'Not Tom,' I salvaged. 'Tom, a tech guy from Pennsylvania. I thought it might be him. He's short-terming with a couple other techies. Renting from—'

'Miss?'

I swallowed, gagged at the smell, stared down at the blood around the cavern in his neck, at the huge black hole in his forehead, the sloppy red circle around his hair like a halo on the floor, at the smashed bone that turned one eye socket into a place where an eyeball hung precariously at the edge.

At the body of Wally, the landlord.

# EIGHTEEN

'Wally?' A man I took to be the scene supervisor prodded.

'Wally . . . the landlord. The curmudgeon.' I shrugged. 'I don't really know him. The short-term tenants may be better. His name'll be on their rental agreements.'

'So how can you be sure about him?'

'I've seen him, spoke, heard the techies refer to him. The woman downstairs mentioned his name.'

'But not his last name?' This from Higgins. Like it was a rare and gauche exclusion. Already the woman was irritating me.

I inhaled slowly, tried for compassion, compromised on just keeping my mouth shut. 'Not his last name.' Even that came out snide.

'You're Lott's sister.'

How long is the statute of limitations on revenge? Higgins wouldn't screw up a case to spite me, but there's a lot of possibility below that level.

'He's retired, right?' By which she meant John, as in 'unable to help you.'

'Got hours of free time.'

Higgins looked like she was balancing her animus against my potential nuisance. She turned to a patrol officer. 'Take her out of here and get her statement.' To me, she added, 'Don't go anywhere.'

The patrol officer – Jameson – and I stepped into the living room. He scanned it for a clear spot where we wouldn't be sideswiped by cops, medics, scene techs, medical examiner's crew racing in and double-timing out. A circle of space with enough room between us for his notepad. He found it in the hall.

'Full name?'

'Darcy Lott.'

'Two t's?'

'Yes.'

'Address?'

While I gave him the standard rundown on living above the zendo, across the hall from the abbot but not 'with' the abbot, I was thinking of Wally. Why would he of all people be shot? He'd probably irritated everyone he'd met in the last half-century, but that wasn't a capital crime. If curmudgeon-ism were a killing offense, the tech companies and realtors wouldn't have to force out long-term tenants: buildings would be empty.

And yet, there he was, shot in the face. In a small room. His killer couldn't have been more than four feet from him. Shot more than once.

His clothes, the same brown ensemble he'd been wearing in the kitchen this afternoon, weren't ripped or wadded. Nothing about them or him suggested a struggle. I could be missing something, but I sure wasn't about to ask my latest cop.

'Phone? And I'll need to see your driver's license. Take it out of the holder . . . please.'

I did. Why Wally? He'd sure made it sound as if there would be no financial advantage in erasing him. Still, a house near the park. It could be paid off.

Or mortgaged to the chimney top.

Or . . . Or . . . I swallowed hard.

I wanted to cry out, 'I'm sorry, Wally. I liked you.' I just felt bad.

I let myself stay there, feeling bad. Not thinking, just feeling the 'bad.'

The cop handed my license back. 'Tell me in your own words how you came upon the deceased.'

'I didn't know it was him. I just figured I might be able to help. Any of the neighbors could have done the same.'

'How is it then, Ms Lott, that you were the one to identify the deceased?'

Truth? Not an option. 'You'll have to ask Officer Santadomingo.'

'Santadomingo?'

'You don't know him? I thought all you guys knew each other?' A cousin of mine from Willits up the coast said that to John at a Thanksgiving dinner years ago. John nearly choked on his drumstick. And then he launched a tedious and very long explanation which could have been condensed into: 'SFPD's a big department.' To Jameson I said, 'He's downstairs. I'll take you to him.'

The stairs were rickety. Jameson, portly enough to make me wonder how he managed the physical, descended with care. He was a step behind me, his exhalations strafing the top of my head with each step. His attention was on the steps he could not see over the expanse of himself.

Mine was on the gun in the lingerie in Mike's apartment. Or not. Minimally, the police would be knocking on Mike's door. As soon as they discovered that Boots, Heather and Tom had been in and out of both units, they'd expand the crime scene to cover the whole building. Once they found the gun, they'd be after Adrienne.

Once they processed fingerprints or tracked her down, they'd be after Mike.

Once they found Mike, who knew? Maybe they'd keep on looking for suspects. Odds were not favorable.

If the gun was back in the lingerie drawer, that would surely narrow their suspects.

For me to get into Mike's apartment would take a miracle. And demonstrate, on my part, an equal mix of daring and stupidity.

I had the key in my pocket. Easy to palm.

Two more stair steps.

I stepped down. Jameson stepped down. My right foot floated out to the right just a bit.

Enough.

He tripped, tumbled on to me. I've done stair falls. I ducked my head and rolled, caught the bottom of the newel post, flung myself to the side to deflect his weight.

'Omigod, are you OK? Officer?'

He said something.

'Hang on. I'll get help. A medic. Don't move.'

I did. I ran out, grabbed a medic, pointed him into the house. 'Hurry. Jameson's down. Bottom of the stairs. Go!'

He was inside before I shut my mouth.

And I was alone.

# NINETEEN

The flashers provided me an instant of cover, turning everything red. Turning my red hair into background. I scrunched down as much as reasonable and was easing toward the back of the crowd when I spotted the trio.

Heather and Tom, his arm around her shoulder, her hand in his butt pocket. Boots next to Tom, holding forth like King Henry VIII to a shorter, thinner sycophant. Tom taking in the scene wide-eyed, following the trajectory of a uniformed officer moving from patrol car into the house. He started toward the house.

Boots grabbed his shoulder, nailing him to the spot. He said something I couldn't hear but knew I agreed with.

Heather leaned into Tom. They looked so couple-on-a-midnight-stroll. So innocuous. So innocent.

Which was dead opposite from how the cops would see me if they got me in an interview booth.

*How is it you happened to be in this building, Ms Lott?*

My response? Spur-of-the-moment lie? Bad choice.

Or, I could go with the truth. Very bad choice.

Or I could turn that innocent trio into a foursome. I slithered over. Boots was muttering something, his right arm extended as he made his point. Slipping under that arm I braced my own against his back. I felt like I could read the man's mind through his back muscles: shock – surprise – pleasure – confusion – reassessment – eyes out for his next move.

'What's going on, guys?'

'Tom had a meet.'

Tom nodded.

'Then we were at our hangout bar on Haight having a beer, hashing it over, and now we're here. But you mean what's going on up there, right?' Heather summarized.

Tom shook his head. Boots hung his arm over my shoulder as he had Heather's a couple hours ago. He paused almost infinitesimally, alert for rejection, and finding none let the weight of his arm sink down. To him and anyone observing he'd sealed me into the two-couples-out-for-a-stroll.

I'd bought some time, but not much. This was cover, not protection. As John had finger-wagged year after year, protection is a stone wall in front of you when a bullet comes. Cover is a car door you can hide behind and hope, until the bullet whips through it into your guts.

Boots eyed the vehicles. 'They must have every officer in town here. Check out the vans.'

'What happened?' Heather asked.

'Wally,' I said. 'He's been shot.'

'Omigod! Really? Why? Shot? Why?'

'You guys were living in there, what do you think?'

Tom shook his head. 'He was a pain, but, to be shot . . .'

'The guy really was a pain. He never saw me without complaining about something. "Don't leave coffee in your cup to spill, Button!" "Put your clothes on your bag, not all over the floor, Boob." "Don't—"'

'Boob?'

'Yeah. Never once got my name right. Did it on purpose; I could tell.'

Tom grinned. 'Yeah, Button, he was playing you.'

'I knew that!' But his arm on my shoulder quivered otherwise.

'Anyway—' Tom was giving him an out – 'bitching 24/7's not a capital crime.'

'It's not like you two didn't have that coming,' Heather said.

Tom looked about to object, glanced down at Heather and eased that into a shrug. 'I guess.'

'Come on, you two have that place like a dumpster.'

'Hey, it's not that bad.'

I watched, stunned at how quickly they eased the focus from their deceased landlord back to themselves. 'Let's talk about this away from here, OK?'

'We can't do that. The police are going to need to talk to us. I mean, we knew Wally.'

Heather gave Tom a poke. 'Everyone knows Wally.'

'Yeah, but maybe we've seen something everybody hasn't. Because we're living with him.'

'You're going to tell the cops he bitches about towels on the bathroom floor?'

'OK, OK. But it's our duty.'

Behind them the scene was slowing. Cops not rushing up steps. Walking down. EMTs standing by their trucks talking. Onlookers easing back, heading out. Voices breaking through the mesh of noise, their words not yet clear.

'Tom,' I said, 'investigators are combing through the apartments, particularly the upstairs. You have things up there?'

'Yeah, sure. But they're not after my clothes.'

'Not clothes . . . Tom.'

He gave his head a shake. 'This is San Francisco! They're dealing with a murder. They're not hauling me in a little stash.'

'They won't bother with it. Unless . . . unless they need to pressure you. There's a lot going on here. They'll want to interview you, but it may not happen right away because, like I say, there's a lot going on. They'll need to get a statement from you. They can't keep innocent witnesses on hold too long. But someone with a little something illegal . . . No rush; you're not going anywhere.'

Heather nodded and turned back to the house, watching the coming and going like a movie preview. She was the swing vote. Say Go and they'd be gone. Say Stay . . . No guy's going to wimp out on a crime scene in front of his girlfriend – his *new* girlfriend.

One of the patrolmen approached a group on the other side of the house. Pad out. Taking names. More than that. Addresses? Connections to the deceased? Santadomingo moved from one man to another, writing down answers. Moving toward us like a breaking wave.

Tom dropped his arm off Heather's shoulder and leapt back. 'My notes are up there! For the solo pres! I've got to get them!'

'Tom, honey, you know your stuff. You don't need notes.'

'I can't blow this! I maxed my cards just to get here. I screw up and I'm back to sweeping up the lab for years. My notes are—'

'Boots can get them for you, right, Boots?'

'Hey, you think I have nothing in the corner of my duffle?'

'Cops hold you, you call your aunt and uncle and they get a big-time lawyer by morning.'

'Hey, what about—'

I'd had enough. 'Stand here any longer and neither of you will be making this decision. I'm outa here.'

'She's right, honey.'

'I can't.'

'Go then. Call me when you get out. If I don't hear from you by morning I'll go to your pres.'

'You?' Tom and Boots said.

'Hey, I've been hearing about this for two days straight. I know it better than you do.'

'Yeah,' Boots said half-laughing. 'They get bored, hit 'em up for leads. Maybe this case will be cold enough for your app.'

'What!' Heather glared.

It was a minute before Boots mumbled, 'Insensitive, huh?'

'You think?' To Tom she said, 'You'll be OK. Trust me.'

Tom didn't. Anyone could tell that. But he kissed her and walked into the house, looking like he was climbing on to the gallows.

When he reached the landing, I strolled off toward Haight, as if I'd seen enough hangings and had a sudden yen for a croissant.

# TWENTY

When I rounded the corner I picked up my pace, turned right toward the park. Where was Mike? He'd left me in the park an hour and a half earlier. He was headed for the car parked across the street from his apartment.

The car was still there, amidst the patrol cars and EMT vans.

Mike had had time to reach the house before Wally was shot. Of course, he hadn't shot him. Of course. He hadn't called the police—

Unless he had. On his new cell phone.

Which meant I didn't dare call that number.

And Mike wouldn't use it to call me.

Which meant . . . I couldn't find him. It meant I was standing in a dark and dangerous park in the middle of the night like a tourist with a pocket full of credit cards.

*What is the price of rice in Luling?* I pictured the old Chinese master Qingyuan shaking his head. *All this speculation! Useless! Useless!*

Mike was not a Buddhist.

*I* was the Buddhist.

Maybe I had let my mind jump to Luling. Maybe . . . the notations on the pad, made by the non-Buddhist, had nothing to do with the koan.

Maybe Qingyuan whacked the monk with his stick and added, '*Don't assume!*'

*Seren *5 Gaté.* Maybe I had assumed too much.

It was an hour before I unlocked the zendo door. When the next thing is getting home after the streetcars and buses have curled up for the night, it's a long run. I had focused on running. After all the tension of the night it had felt good to just run, full out on some blocks, easy on others.

When I climbed up the stairs to my room I knew what to do. It wasn't magic, just common sense. I checked messages on the landline. Zip. It was 2.42 a.m. With luck I'd get four hours of sleep. I headed for the bathroom.

Taped on the mirror was a note from Leo: *Sleep In!*

*Thursday*

'Who the hell are you?' Adrienne's Ferente's eyes were glued half shut. In a bathrobe that was a mix of pink flowers and wrinkles, she peered out through the barely opened doorway. Her chin-length hair, which had probably looked smart and stylish the night before, now stuck out stiff in divergent directions like one of those exotic fruits you don't know where to start peeling. She could have posed for 'morning after.' It was 9:00 a.m. She looked like 6:00.

I felt like 4:00. 'Darcy Lott. Mike's sister.' I pushed my way into her flat.

'Mike told you where I am?'

Not hardly! But I wasn't about to tell her that.

The place was a basement of a cottage set behind an auto body shop in Berkeley. The gate beside the cottage, led to a cement path and around back. If the dented old car out front belonged to Adrienne, maybe she was hoping the body shop guys would pound it out by mistake. Dimples and pockmarks covered both front fenders and the passenger side rear, but the more serious gouges disfigured the front right. The passenger mirror had been knocked off, leaving only rusted holes. I bent closer. But, of course, time and wind had blown away traces of anything foreign.

The house was off Sorrento Way between San Pablo and Kains Avenues in the Berkeley flatlands.

*Seren *5 Gate.*

*Kains!* Not koan!

*Sorrento*, not Serenity.

*Not S5 or K5. Not the number 5 at all, but S.P! San Pablo, San Pablo Avenue. The long-time commercial route that parallels the freeway.*

Sorrento, between Kains and San Pablo. So short and obscure it was only that one block long. No arrow or street number indicating the basement unit. Visitors had to know to go through the gate.

*Through the gate.* Not *gaté, gaté*, the ending line of chants. Gone, gone, gone beyond . . .

The indentations on the pad were not a koan that made no sense, but an abbreviated address written in a hurry by a person who needed to find it. Talk about tunnel vision! When this was all over and we Lotts were all safe and sitting around the kitchen table, the rest of them would roast me! They'd say—

But I'd have plenty of time to hear their snide-isms.

Now, at least, I'd found the house.

In the body shop, a machine roared. The walls here probably didn't truly shake but it felt like they were in danger of crumbling. Her flat in San Francisco wasn't large, but it had charm. The kitchen was like Wally's with a built-in china cabinet. The stove was gas – a plus until the day before yesterday. The fridge had rounded corners and a blue light at the top, the kind of thing people have had chugging along in their vacation homes for decades. The living room had that bay window.

And the bedroom had the gun. But I'd get to that later.

This place wasn't so much a room in a basement as a basement with a sofa too decrepit to be used upstairs and too heavy to haul to the curb. A faux-wood desk of the same vintage. The 'kitchen' was a gray basement sink, the kind you wash off grease in, the refrigerator an under-the-counter affair, the kind you keep beer in, and the stove a two-ring hot plate. The window looked out on garbage cans.

'Couldn't you have found something better?'

'On two-day notice? Scoring this was a coup.'

Something banged. Maybe a truck sliding off a hoist. Adrienne didn't even look up. She ran her knuckles across her eyes and we both understood that only the slow reactions from a sleepless night had kept her from shutting the door when she first saw me.

I said, 'Wally's dead.'

'What?' She blinked a few times to bring his demise into focus. 'You woke me up to tell me that? How'd you even find me? No one knows I'm here. It's just for a few days.'

'I managed. Answer my questions and I'll be history.'

She pushed herself up. 'I don't have to—'

'Your landlord was killed right above your apartment. You

wanted to be elsewhere so bad that you chose to live here. Police might find that . . .' I paused '. . . odd.'

She leaned forward, opened her mouth to protest and then sighed and sat back.

'How long have you rented from Wally?'

'Ten years.'

'Was he working back then?'

'Working? He never worked.'

'He's not a trust fund baby. Where'd he get money?'

'I don't know.'

'Think. You lived there ten years; no one's going to believe you never wondered. The police were all over his apartment last night. If they haven't gotten to yours already, they will. And to you. Even here. Even if I don't alert them. So, Adrienne, what did you notice about him?'

She ran her fingers through her hair, raking clumps downward with no set destination, as if she was trying to pull her mind into focus by her hair. 'Coffee shops. It was like he lived in coffee shops and visited the apartment.'

'Which coffee shop? If you're a serious coffee drinker, you find your best place and become a regular. You claim your table. Your order becomes "the usual". You don't lower yourself to drink lesser coffee in lesser establishments.'

'Not him. I saw him in the old place near Ashbury, the one that was next to the head shop that was there forever, and then all of a sudden it was a Gap. He was in Starbucks, in McDonald's. In the Bottomless Cup. You know, everywhere.'

'Was he meeting someone?'

'Yeah, but no one special. And special people. I saw him with our district supervisor; with the mayor once, but just because the mayor had been our district sup before. When I first moved in, Wally was still in the mix. Things have thinned out by now.'

'And? Women?'

'Women?' From the baffled look on her face I could have been asking about individual Shiba Inus or emissaries from Saturn. 'Women? Not much. Wow, dead,' she said, as if that word was just now hardening into reality. 'I never expected that of Wally. Shot?'

I hadn't mentioned shooting. 'Through his head. From the front. Not random. Shot more than once.'

Sirens squealed on San Pablo Avenue. The avenue was a major connector, a straight route for police, fire, EMTs. She must have been jolted up ten times during the night. This made the eleventh.

'So, Adrienne, he mostly met men in coffeehouses. Was he gay?'

'Wally? I doubt it. He was like . . . sex wasn't his deal.'

'So what was?'

She shrugged.

'Oh come on. You lived there ten years and you've never once wondered? I don't believe that. The police'll ask you and they won't believe you either.'

'Whatever it was, he kept it to himself. I mean, he never had guests, unless you call his weekend renters guests. You know their ads say, those places that set up the rentals. "Be a guest in the house of . . ." That kind of schmaltz.'

'Otherwise, no one? Ever?'

'Not that I saw. I wasn't watching or anything. But I'd've heard something if there'd been people up there. I made the mistake one weekend of staying when he was renting out his sofa and it was like the sofa guy was tap-dancing. Never'll do that again.'

'Mail? Packages? Deliveries?'

'Boxes? Never. But mail, yeah.' She leaned forward, suddenly near awake. 'Wally never said anything, but the man was obsessive about his mail. He was always home when it came. Always watching the box.'

'For?'

'I don't know. He never bounded down the stairs.'

I couldn't imagine Wally bounding anywhere, and from her expression neither could she. 'Did he rip open letters at the box?'

'Are you kidding? Never. It was like there were eyes in the walls.'

'But he checked who they were from?'

'Oh yeah.'

'Did they come around the first of the month? Or the end?'

She was sitting up now, alert, or almost, and she seemed to be kneading the questions, her fingers moving in and out. 'No, no special time. It was more like they were gifts, you know? Random gifts.'

'Did he seem happy to get them?'

'Wally? Happy? I never saw him without a scowl. He would have grumbled through sex. Except, like I said, he couldn't be bothered with sex.'

'How about calls? Texts?'

'Nothing I heard. He wasn't a nose to phone in the crosswalks type. He was, you know, an old guy. The guys he'd be sitting with in cafes were old guys, mostly.'

'Mostly?'

'Maybe three out of four.'

'The others?'

'You're asking if there was a commonality? Uh-uh. None. Not race – some Hispanic; a couple blacks but not together. Never together. He was always one on one.'

'Like an interview?'

'Maybe. But it wasn't like he was all private about it. He's lived here forever. Everyone knew him. He'd be cordial – well, cordial for him – if you passed his table. Not "sit down a while" cordial. And really, no one was desperate for that.'

'Everybody knew him?' I repeated questioningly. 'And you?'

'I made a point of not knowing.'

'Because?'

'I've got a good deal with the flat.'

'What do you pay?'

'Depends on his short-termers. Months they're there, I sail free.'

'Nothing? That is a good deal.' No wonder she was willing to endure this place. 'Wally . . . What's his last name?'

'Last name? I don't know.'

'What do you write on your rent checks?'

'I pay in cash. OK, here's what I figured on that. These short-term renters, they pay a bundle for a week or weekend. They sleep on everything that's horizontal. Some of them would sleep standing up if that's all there was. Whatever. Wally rakes it in on them. He can't make them all pay cash. So there's a record of their rent, his income. The IRS could get that if they went after him. But me, he can do in cash. With all he gets from them, the feds aren't going to imagine there's even more rent money they've missed.'

'Still, a small deception.'

'Wally's a small deception guy.'

'Which means?'

'Just that. He likes to be in control, not take chances, not get taken. An old guy who's always checking his wallet.'

I nodded. Standing on the sidewalk, checking to be sure he wouldn't be sideswiped by not having enough cash. Never looking up in time to see the mugger.

'He was so careful, and yet he's dead.'

'You get old, you get used to being safe. You check your wallet, but you forget to check your back.' She could have been talking about a minor character in a movie. I eyed her more carefully trying to suss out if that was true, mostly true, or partly. Ten years living beneath a man, knowing him well enough to list off his hangouts, is a long time to have no emotion when you hear he's dead.

She braced her hands on the edge of the sofa but didn't exert the effort to push herself up yet. 'So, you done? I could be sleeping.'

*Fat chance. I didn't track you down only to leave without finding out about Mike.* 'Tell me again how you came to offer the apartment to my brother.'

'He called.'

'He had your number?'

'Obviously. He called me.'

'You and Mike were, uh, friends?'

'What?'

'How is it you know my brother? Are you friends? More than friends? Are—'

'A. We're not friends. B. If we had been before he offered me this dump, we wouldn't be now.'

'So, how'd he get your number?'

'Wally gave it to him.'

'Wally?'

'That's what he said, your fine brother.'

'How would he know Wally?' I was thinking aloud more than asking her. But she said, 'Maybe he met him in a coffee shop. Any time in the last fifty years – that's what somebody or other said. When Wally left college he just moved his butt from the lecture hall to the coffee shops.'

'So, you're saying Mike ran into him there this year?'

'Are you listening? I don't know. I don't know your brother outside of one phone call and the key under the mat. He said he'd stayed here from time to time. That it was safer than it looked.' She laughed. 'That should have been the clue.'

'And the gun in your lingerie drawer?'

'You were poking through my underwear!' She shot up off the sofa; stood, hands actually on hips, and glared down at me. For an instant I was amazed she had that much energy. She stomped to the door, yanked it open. 'Get out!'

I didn't move. 'Your gun?'

'I don't own a gun. Not now. Not last week.'

'But, there is a gun, in your bedroom. You can stonewall me, but like I keep telling you, the police will get to your apartment. They'll open every drawer. They'll find that handgun and they'll end up sitting right here where I am, asking you exactly what I'm asking. And, Adrienne, they won't leave.' I let that bit of reality sink in, then said, 'Whose gun is it?'

I thought she'd opt for the mysterious housesitter, Mike, but she leaned back against the doorjamb and began tapping her finger on a knuckle of her other hand. In the garage out front metal clanked, an engine roared, brakes squealed, engine roared again. The odor of gas wafted through this basement, though maybe I was imagining that.

'I'm still furious about you rooting through my drawers . . .'

'Sorry,' I said. 'Really.'

'Huh? Yeah, OK.'

'You were about to say . . .?'

'Wally. It's probably Wally's gun. He's got these strangers, these tech guys, and who knows how weird they are? They sign up online – I know that because he bitched about it, having no idea who he'd get. I don't know if their conferences or anyone screens these guys, but to hear Wally – and you've got to consider the source there; Wally'd bitch asking for a glass of water. Anyway, to hear him he could be housing a bunch of crazies. So, it'd make sense for him to buy a gun. And since he's renting out his flat, it'd make sense to stash the gun in mine.'

We were still a moment, both realizing, whatever Wally had thought, he'd been wrong and he was dead.

I stood. 'Thanks for you help. Here's my card. In case . . .'

She slipped it in the pocket of her robe, where it would probably disintegrate in the wash.

'The people in the house upstairs? Are they the owners?'

She laughed, an edgy sound, and pulled the door open wider. 'Hardly. This property doesn't look like much. It isn't much. But it's in Berkeley. If you own property like this, here, you don't have to live in it. You sit on the beach in Mexico and cash the checks.'

'Thanks,' I repeated just in case. If she'd connected me with the owner, that would have been a boon. But property ownership was public record.

My phone rang just as I pulled into traffic. I let it go to message.

# TWENTY-ONE

'Mike had a crash pad in Berkeley. You knew that, right?'

'Nooo.'

I'd heard that single syllable – meaning not-no, maybe not-yes – from my sister, Janice, as long as I could remember. Janice is the number three child in our bunch of seven. The one who never fit. Katie, now Katharine on the newspaper masthead, was already writing in kindergarten, investigating chocolate pudding thefts, joining clubs, running clubs, getting awards. John was destroying robbers in the backyard before nursery school. Word is that Gary shot out of the birth canal objecting and never stopped. Gary and Gracie (the epidemiologist who'd been known as the bug kid) were a pair; different foci but they always had each other's backs.

Like Mike and me.

Which left Janice.

Janice, 'the nice one.' The one left holding the bag and sneered at for doing it. The one afraid to turn her back because she knew no one had it. Katie, John and Janice are so much older than me that they were out of the house before I was in middle school. Most of what I know about Janice is family lore and not flattering. Her final indictment in the eyes of my fourth-generation San Francisco family was her move to Berkeley.

Citizens of other states may link the two cities together, but locals know the difference. Berkeleyans appreciate the value of their time, their long-term civic concern for the rights of the individual, their environmental probity. (The first integrated schools in the country were in Berkeley.) They talk about San Franciscans having a 'hard energy.' San Franciscans cannot believe any sane person could live in the best city in the world and opt to move to the suburbs. The City and County of San Francisco is 49 square miles at the tip of a peninsula. In their eyes the water keeps the bourgeoisie out.

I could go on, I thought, as I waited for Janice to modify her *no*, but I'd heard John and Gary and Gracie riff on it all too often. When I moved away to New York none of them complained. San Francisco . . . Paris . . . Rome . . . London . . . New York, OK. A volitional move to San Jose, Los Angeles, San Diego, Berkeley? It was akin to six-to-life in Atascadero.

She pushed a clump of fading brown hair behind her ear, as if shoving it out of sight for a visitor. 'Can I make you some tea?'

I would have killed for coffee. Not likely here. 'When Mike was missing all those years, you were the one who knew where he was.'

'Where he'd *been*.'

Big difference, but I wasn't going to give her that.

'I tried to make him—'

'You were the one who never let on, Janice. The one who let us all look over the railing and think the worst every time we drove over the Golden Gate Bridge.'

'Nobody told me.'

'"Nobody tells me anything." That could be your name.'

I stared not at her but past her into the paper-cluttered living room of this flat in the hills. She could have countered with: you would have done the same thing for Mike. And she'd have been right. I'd destroyed a marriage searching for him.

I was desperate to avoid looking at her, to not see her shrink back against my betrayal. When I'd been stranded she was the one I'd called. And yet, little as I really knew my sister, I did know this. She was concealing something. Throwing out answers that were not whole, running diversions, protecting the nugget of I-couldn't-guess-what, as if it would blow up in her face. She'd been a rabbit raised with foxes; she knew how to hide in plain sight. 'Mike had a crash pad in Berkeley. You knew that, right?'

'No!' She grabbed my shoulder and slammed me into the wall.

My head ricocheted off the plaster. For a moment my vision went blurry. I couldn't feel my fingers at all. I stared at her pale blue eyes. I was too shocked to speak. The teenage lore of Janice is that she took it and took it and took it until one day Gary found her cringing behind the water heater and she came at him with a knife.

'No.' Her energy drained as fast as it had built.

I wondered if I'd imagined the whole thing.

'No.' Her voice quavered. 'Why would he? He could stay here any time.' She was staring at my shoulder, rubbing it now as if to erase her outburst. 'Why would he need somewhere else?'

'Women?'

'Not that place. If he took a woman there she wouldn't be thinking about him, she'd be looking out for rats.'

She knew she'd blown it the instant the words left her mouth. I just shook my head. Then I smiled and patted her arm. She had husbanded secrets about Mike for years, never letting on to the family, not even to Mom. It was, she told me later, the reason she'd had to move out of the city. 'I should be pleased you let your guard down with me.' I repeated the question. 'Why did he need a place to stay here when he could have dropped in on you?'

She sighed.

'To do something he didn't want you to know?'

'I put my life on hold for him. How can he . . .?'

'It's the question we all have. Here, sit.' I steered her to the sofa and waited while she moved a pile of orange flyers to the floor. Monday, on the pier, I'd promised Mike my silence. Screw it. 'Janice, I need you to keep this to yourself.'

'My superpower.' She almost smiled.

I gave her the rundown. 'So he left his own place to stay in the Haight with Wally—'

'Wally Ellis?'

'You know him?'

'Everybody knew him.'

*Knew?* 'You already know he's dead?'

'What? No way! Wally?'

I told her about that, too. 'So, Janice, Mike tells Adrienne about this dive in Berkeley.'

'He leaves his place because it's too dangerous and goes to Wally's and Wally is shot. Did someone mistake Wally for Mike?'

I almost laughed. 'Not if they're of our species. Other than sex and race there's no similarity at all.'

Janice picked up the flyers and started batting at the edges, thinking. In the years of her exile here she had kept herself in the counterculture 'know' in case she heard something about Mike. She'd been to meetings. Many meetings. She'd probably straightened more packs of flyers than the rest of the family combined. Now as I looked at her, I could see her puzzling out what these last days meant, the way she would have assessed news of an anti-coal-tar demonstration in Canada that might possibly have attracted Mike. Tapping, mulling, finding the sheet of the story that didn't fit.

I waited, noting how focused my sister was, how in her element. How relaxed.

'You know what surprises me most?' she said, still tapping but so softly that none of the papers moved. 'Not that Wally Ellis was killed, but that he was killed now. Years ago he was the source. He knew everyone. All hush-hush went through him. The mayor wanted the lowdown on a gang lord, Wally was the one with the real scoop. Reporter wanted the rumors on a parish priest, he could save himself weeks of work by one coffee with Wally. Everybody knew Wally; Wally knew everything. "Gave the least amount", that's the phrase I kept hearing. He gave to get. It was the getting he cared about. So, he was sitting on a lot, always. Or so it seemed. If he'd been shot back then there would have been a hundred suspects.'

'So no one could take the chance?'

'Exactly. He was a master of self-protection. Ironic, huh? He never revealed anything about someone who could hurt him, but to stay in the game he had to give something.'

'So giving up the secrets of the dead was safe?'

'The dead and the long-missing. Wally used to laugh that he was an occasional guest columnist at all the underground rags. He wrote almost in code. You really had to know what he was talking about to know what he was saying.'

'The long-missing? He wrote about Mike?'

'Not by name. Trust me, Darcy, even you wouldn't have recognized Mike. Wally wasn't "giving," he was just putting out teasers, telling the probably six people who bothered to read him that he was open for chat.'

Janice was still bent over the flyers but her whole posture had changed from the wary near-crouch when she'd opened the door to me. I could make out only a bit of her face but I was sure it had morphed into the chairman of the board. 'And then?'

'He just became less relevant. His sources aged out. They died. Computers, texts, electronics he didn't know. He sort of got put out to pasture.'

'He still went to cafes.'

'Drinking coffee is not the same as hearing dirt.'

Now I did laugh. Janice looked up – as if surprised – and laughed herself. In that moment I saw her as she might have been, if the wind had been at her back.

I handed her a pile of flyers. 'You know, Janice, you are the best at what you do. You have led me down a detour, sure, but one that's valuable. You've done it so successfully – that's your superpower – that I almost forgot that you are hiding something. You're always hiding something, aren't you? Hey, don't bother to tear up. All of us Lotts have our superpowers. Well, I'm the one who doesn't give up. What are you not telling me?'

She went mute.

I'd forgotten that hideout of hers.

'So why would Wally be killed now?'

'Maybe he got careless, though I haven't heard that, a little looser-lipped with age. I don't know.'

She said it without hesitation. I believed her. Which meant that was not what she was hiding.

'Are you sure you don't want tea?'

Oh yeah. 'Thanks.'

'Mint? Chamomile? Green?'

'Black.'

She hesitated, but only momentarily, before virtually levitating off the sofa and flying into the kitchen to boil water and hunt in the back of the cabinet for a bag of caffeinated tea she might have bought a decade ago.

I shifted to keep her in view while I sifted through our conversation.

'Mike *had* a crash pad in Berkeley. At a time he couldn't stay with you. There's no need for him to have it now. If he made use of it now he'd be sleeping there instead of giving it to Adrienne.'

Despite the hiss of the heating water I heard her gasp.

'Adrienne said he'd stayed there from time to time. He had a hideout here . . . before. While he was missing, right? During the time I thought he might be dead, he had access to this basement in Berkeley, right?' I stamped into the kitchen. 'Right, Janice?'

'I didn't know.'

'Yeah, sure.'

'No, really.'

'I'm supposed to believe that? From you, the queen of secrets?'

The water was boiling, steam squealing from the spout. She ignored it. She looked at me, her eyes suddenly seeming a darker blue. 'I was trying to keep a loose rein on him while he was gone. To be sure he wasn't dead. Sometimes I discovered where he had just been, sometimes I was a year behind. But we were never in contact.'

I turned off the water and waited.

'No really, Darcy, if he and I were in touch, if he trusted me, why would he come to Berkeley and not come here?'

'Danger?'

She shrugged.

'How long have you known about this basement of his?'

She looked down at her watch. 'Half an hour.'

Maybe. Maybe months, years longer. But that was a detour I wasn't trotting down. Not now. 'OK. Do your stuff. Let's dig up the landlord and see just how long our missing brother was dropping into town.'

*While letting us wonder if he was dead.* My whole body went rigid. I had to brush away that thought; I couldn't even consider it.

*While I stayed away from San Francisco because I couldn't bear the constant reminders.*

*While Gracie wrapped herself in work.*

*While Gary wrapped himself in marriages and divorces.*

*While Mom never left overnight lest Mike came home and found the house empty.*

*During that time Mike came through Berkeley, fifteen miles from home.*

Whatever his reason I couldn't deal with it, not now. I focused on Janice pulling up the lid of the computer. Focused on screens without reading words. At one point I said, 'Adrienne told me the landlord could be in Mexico.'

Facing the computer keys, Janice was like a concert pianist, head jutting forward, hanging off her spine like the whole thing was a question mark. So focused she didn't hear her audience of one holding her breath. And when she sat up straight a couple minutes later, she had that look of transcendence. 'Maybe he gets his burritos at a Guadalajara,' she said, 'but he gets his mail outside Point Arena.'

Up the coast, in the abalone diving area.

'He?'

'Mountain Properties.'

'That means nothing.'

'That's the point. Not a dead end, but not an open door.' She closed the computer. 'Drink your tea. I'll drive. It's a long drive and your eyelids are resting on your cheek bones.'

It took me a moment to adjust to my transformed sister. To even think of consuming the tea I'd suggested only as busy work for her. Now I added milk and enough sugar – raw, of course – to shoot my lids into my eyebrows. I figured I had three hours before they crashed back down into my incisors. What I needed was time to think.

I could sleep in the car. Think behind my lowered lids. Company would be comforting. Someone to have my back.

But there was something more pressing. 'Mike's car. I parked it across from Wally's. If the cops—'

She held out her hand for the keys. 'You can check your phone while I change.'

But before I could check, the phone rang.

'It's Mom,' I called to Janice.

'Hi hon,' Mom said, as she frequently did, and then had to stop to remember which of her daughters she'd called. Her normal words. But her tone was not normal at all. For a moment I thought she really had lost track of whether she was leaving a message for Gracie or Katie or even Janice. She sounded as close to tears as I could remember since Dad died. 'I'm going to have to miss the movie tonight. Everything's OK,' she said, as if hearing how completely her voice belied that. As if forgetting it wasn't me she had plans with. 'The thing is Duffy . . .' An eternity passed while she swallowed so loud I could hear her throat gurgle, while she pulled herself together enough to explain about the Scottie who had been my dog in New York until he set foot in Mom's house.

I'd watched them, a few months after I moved back to the city; Duffy had been staying with Mom until I could make arrangements to take him. Duffy, the formerly condescending terrier, rubbing against her leg after accepting a ruffling of his fur. Duffy, I realized, my *former* dog. It wasn't so much what she did, as it was the softening of her face when she offered him a piece of beef from her plate, the way she patted her newly reupholstered sofa and waited for him to leap up. It was as if the black Scottish terrier was the embodiment of 'Mike is back. The dark time is over and things are all right.'

'Duffy . . .' she squeaked out, 'I saw someone in a slicker tossing something. Turned out to be meatballs laced with bug killer. Tossing them by the dunes where I take Duffy. There are other dogs there, you know that, right? Duffy likes to see other dogs but he doesn't give them more than a perfunctory sniff. You know what a furry little snob he is—'

'Mom!'

'Darcy, a beagle died. Kory, the girl who owns the Great Dane told me. They rushed him to the vet but it was too late. It was awful.'

'Duffy! He didn't eat it, did he? Is he—'

'Duffy had a bad night.'

'But he's OK now?'

'Poor little guy was actually moaning. The vet wanted to keep him there but I couldn't leave him like that. I was up all night. It's not easy to keep a hot-water bottle on a dog's stomach.'

In case I ever wondered why my dog had abandoned me for Mom.

'Is he OK now?'

'Still off his food. I soft-boiled an egg and he did eat that. But I don't want to leave him alone now. I know you understand, hon.'

I nodded. I couldn't trust myself to speak. If something had happened to Duffy . . . I . . .

If something *else* happened to Duffy, I couldn't bear the thought of Mom watching him die.

If someone wanted to hurt us, they couldn't have planned it better.

# TWENTY-TWO

I was dropping Janice at BART. Faster, she said, to get into the city. She'd switch to a streetcar – good, she said, for her to practice on the city transit. Then, with relief, she'd pick up Mike's car and drive like a normal suburban woman to Mom's. And would not open the door to anyone except one of the family. It didn't seem like precaution enough. Nothing did. I left a message for John to call Janice. Wherever he was, no matter how out of contact he might say he'd be, John would check messages. He'd be certain that in an emergency only he could save us. That had driven me crazy since I was old enough to use two syllable words. But now . . . Even so I was sweating when I pulled up by the Honda. 'Don't go out at all,' I said as Janice reached for the door of Gary's Aston Martin.

'Darcy, you're overreacting. How could the poisoner be sure Duffy would go to the beach that day, that he'd be the dog—'

'Even worse!'

'You're being—'

'Maybe so. But first Mike, then Gracie gets hit. Then Gary's garage. Now this. This guy is circling us. If you have any way of contacting Mike—'

'I don't. I told you.'

She had. 'Promise me you won't take Duffy out of the house. Not even the front yard. Especially—' oh, God! – 'the yard. Don't go to the store. If there's not enough food, order take-out.'

'What? A dog food burrito?'

'Yeah, right. I'll call Jansen's.'

I put a restraining hand on her arm. 'Jansen's Burritos. What made you think of them?' Mike and I had gone there years ago, before he disappeared. I'd told Leo about those trips, when the Perezes let me work the line like I was a regular employee, not a child.

I'd told Leo because Jansen's Burritos had popped into my mind during zazen.

I'd thought of it then because Mike had mentioned it on the pier.

But none of that had I told Janice. I waited. But she just shook her head. 'Did Mike mention it?'

'Probably. Who else?'

'Recently?'

'No.'

'And yet you came out with the name.'

She nodded, hesitated, then admitted, 'I don't know.'

'Never mind. Have John get take-out from where the cops eat.'

I don't know what I expected at Jansen's Burritos, but it had to be more than this abandoned building. Rumor had it that the single garage-sized building was an earthquake shack. From the looks of the decrepit and tiny detached building, it could have been. Or more likely it wasn't. Historical societies would have snapped up a relic of the city's great catastrophe over a hundred years ago. They would have moved the little wooden tent-substitute to a place of honor amidst photographs of lines of them in the sand of Golden Gate Park, with serious-minded survivors cooking soup in the open and making plans to rebuild the city bigger and better.

Still, I wouldn't have bet my last toe on it being less than a century old. The sign – JANSEN'S BURRITOS – itself could have weathered a hundred winters. The letters were so faded that I wondered if the place was deserted. I hadn't been here since I was a child. In my memory there was always a line out the door and down the sidewalk past the driveway and in front of the house next door.

Now, though, grass grew untrampled. The huge garbage cans that lined the side were gone. I walked down the alley without the cans, to the back where Senora Perez had allowed herself three minutes off each hour. Doctor's orders, her son Enrique announced.

'*Three* minutes?' I'd asked.

'"A few minutes," the doctor ordered. Mama nodded like she

understood.' Enrique had laughed then. Senora Perez was too busy to learn another language, she'd always insisted. She cooked; *they* – Enrique, Maria, and Sonja – could talk. 'Mama asked me what "a few" meant. I said, "More than a couple."'

He'd told me while I was stirring the newly poured black beans in the tray, and Senora Perez, who didn't understand English, but understood enough, laughed so hard she had to turn away from the stove.

There had been an Adirondack chair out there, green. Now tan grass waved in the wind and the fog, which showed no sign of lifting today, turned the whole scene sepia. It looked like Senora Perez had never sat here. Like no one had for years.

With all the irony I could muster in unvoiced words I thought: Maybe, just maybe, I was making too much of the burrito connection. Maybe the burritos were just beans and rice in a tortilla.

I walked slowly back to the sidewalk. I had hoped that the Perezes or Mr Jansen would give me a name, a lead, an *ah-ah!* about Mike. A Saint Christopher's medal to find his secrets. Now I couldn't even find them. It had been a stupid idea. I'd wasted an hour. I could have been—

The koan! *Don't get caught up in the price of rice in Luling! Don't drift into fantasy. Focus here, now.*

I inhaled, and looked around this block I hadn't seen in years. Back then it had been a warehouse neighborhood in the outer Mission. Now there were still square buildings without windows, but two across the street sported *sold* signs. It wasn't the historical society that would be eyeing the shack, but developers. Small as the shack and lot was, it would hold three or four one-bedroom 'luxury' apartments piled one atop another.

The building next door was another prime spot, still single-family with a porch. A developer could do a spit and polish and flip it for a near-mil profit, regardless of what he paid the owner. And if the owner was the same man who'd been there years ago, who'd bought the place for less than an electric car now, the profit would be all the greater.

I was knocking on the door before I remembered the man. The groucho, the Perezes had called him behind his back.

'Yeah?'

The groucho had grayed but not mellowed. 'I was here years ago, when I was a kid.'

'So?'

So much for pleasantries.

'I'm looking for the Perezes. Or Mr Jansen.'

'Dead.'

'All of them?'

'Jansen.'

'Wow! He was what, like forty when I knew him. Buff. Serious about being buff.'

Groucho shrugged. 'Didn't save him.'

'Save him? How did he die?'

His hand went to the door. 'Who's asking?'

'Darcy Lott. I used to come here with my brother. You used to snarl at us.'

'I snarled at everyone. Jansen and his flock . . . Smell morning and night. People – you and your *brother* – on my sidewalk, pissed – *pissed off!* – if I walked across my own sidewalk to my own door!'

'Not me, Groucho—'

'Groucho!' He glared from under his awning of gray eyebrows. Then he guffawed. 'Didn't know I knew, did you? The flock, they thought it was their secret. Like I cared what they called me.'

'So, Mr . . .'

'Marcus.' He laughed so hard the gray stubble that covered his head bounced. 'Groucho Marcus!'

I thought he was going to choke. His face was a collection of balls – cheeks, nose, full-lipped mouth and bags under the eyes so large they bounced – and all an eerie shade of maroon. He was so like Wally Ellis I felt like I was talking to a ghost. And yet he wasn't quite the same. Not the same pale skin. His was olive. More hair. About the same age, but when Wally was ruining his posture leaning over tables in coffee shops to add to his gossip collection, this man might have been lifting weights in his back room. (I couldn't picture him in an actual gym.) And unlike Wally, whose complaints had boiled over like unwatched noodles on the stove, he seemed to begrudge every extra syllable.

'Mr Marcus—'

'Grouch,' he coughed out. 'It's what my friends call me.'

*You have friends!* But I caught myself in time. What I said was, 'Mr Jansen, how did he die?'

'I don't know. But I'll tell you this, like you said, he was a healthy guy. He musta made a mint on that stand, and I never saw him lift a finger. Resta them worked like slaves—'

*Guess Marcus can boil over, too.*

'You said you worked there—'

'Helped. I was twelve.'

'They had kids that young. They all worked. 'Cept him.'

'I remember that. My brother and I used to talk about that.'

'What'd this brother of yours think?'

'Said Jansen married well.'

'You can say that again.'

'"He was a healthy guy," you were saying . . .'

'Yeah, yeah.' Grouch stepped back inside the doorjamb. 'He was always there, in charge. Guy coulda had a clipboard the way he marched around that place, you know what I mean?'

'I do.'

'Then one day he wasn't there. And the next day the lot of them were gone. Left everything. Pots, dishes, paper plates and napkins still in the garbage cans inside. Place stank. Flies! When I spotted the rats I called the health department.'

'When they came, did you go inside?'

'You kidding? They put on masks.'

'Weren't you curious?'

'Not enough to fight the rats. But I watched. They didn't call the cops. No cops, no ambulance. So, no one inside. That's it!'

'"That's it?" Didn't you wonder about them? Try to find out?'

'What was I going to do, drive across the border to Tijuana and go knocking on doors? Ask if anyone in Mexico knows a Perez family?'

Point taken. 'What about Jansen?'

He shrugged. 'Who was I going to ask?'

I felt like the noodle pot lifted off the burner. This couldn't be a dead end. It just couldn't! I said, 'What about the abalone?'

'What about it?' The words were a brush-off, but his tone was a tease.

'What do you know?'

'I've got time. Might be something up there I recognize.'

'What exactly?'

'Won't know till I see it.' He eyed my fine car. 'Ride in the country? I got nothing better to do.'

# TWENTY-THREE

If John was answering, I'd have texted him about this trip north with Grouch Marcus. I did text Mike, but got no response. I might have had second thoughts. But Grouch Marcus was the only chance of a lead I had.

I grabbed a double espresso at Renzo's Caffe – half for the coffee, and half to show him Grouch. If it had been Wally Ellis instead of Grouch, he and Renzo would still be there, both of them bent forward over the counter, dealing from their stash of connections and secrets and San Francisc-ablia like card sharks. But Grouch Marcus seemed to have nothing to give and no interest in hanging around.

I headed for the Golden Gate. If taking Grouch Marcus with me to the abalone area was a bad idea, I'd have hours to regret it. I'd hoped Renzo, who collected knowledge of people, would have a snippet on Marcus, but he didn't. It embarrassed him. It unnerved me. At least, I thought, someone knows where I'm headed and whom I taking.

'That Renzo,' Marcus said, leaning back against the leather seat of my lawyer brother's show-'em-who-they're-dealing-with sedan. The four-door Aston Martin proclaimed, in its subdued and wildly expensive British elegance, that its driver was a man only a fool would oppose.

I'd done my share of car gags, but if a stunt double's driving, the car's a junker. We don't spin out in quarter-of-a-million-dollar sedans. Gary got his show-'ems used, so make that a hundred thou and change.

The wheel was on the right. I'd let my hair down and now, as I accelerated on to the Golden Gate, long, curly red strands blew through the window and drivers in the slow lanes stared. I could get used to this.

'That Renzo,' Marcus repeated, 'he's a grumpy bastard.'

This from a guy nicknamed Groucho. About a man on a first-name basis with half the city. But I understood Marcus's viewpoint.

I'd asked Renzo about Jansen's Burritos and he'd come up empty. It galled him. I'd shot a glance at Marcus, quick enough to see his mouth tighten before he faux-coughed.

Still, his dissing my friend Renzo got to me. 'If there's anything to unearth about Jansen's, Renzo will dig it up. He knows everyone.'

By now Renzo would be canvassing all friends, acquaintances, and barely knowns within a square mile of the old Jansen's Burritos. With luck my cell would ring before I reached the rainbow tunnel. I could quiz Marcus, but better to do it when I got the right questions.

Every few minutes my eyes did a three point – road, rearview, road and rest there – checking for a tail that could be Mike. Not expecting to spot him. Not spotting him. He could be following me. He could be anywhere.

When I headed into the rainbow arch of the Waldo Tunnel, now officially the Robin Williams Tunnel, I altered my hope to: phone would ring before I reached Petaluma. And that to Guerneville . . . Jenner by the sea. And then the connection failed. Maybe it had failed earlier. Maybe I'd just hit a dead spot. I'd taken it easy on the freeway and through the little towns along the Russian River, but now on the tight curves of Route 1, by the cliffs above the sea, I played the gas against the drag, braked hard, rode the corners. Marcus was good; he didn't gasp, but he couldn't keep himself from grabbing onto whatever he could find.

I said, 'Tell me about Jansen.'

'I gave you what I knew.'

'Oh come on. You're hanging out on your porch, next door to a guy who's strolling around doing nothing. Of course you're going to talk.'

'Me? Not chatty.'

*True dat!* 'You, not curious? You'd have to be dead to not want to know his deal.'

'I keep my distance.'

'I was there, Grouch. I saw you with him.' Not true, but could have been.

He didn't respond.

Ahead was a short downhill ending in a sharp right curve. I

pressed the gas till the engine roared. As we hit the curve I turned toward him. It was a trick I learned doing a gag in LA, the head-turn while eyes stay just enough on the road. The maneuver had seemed flawed to me, but when I saw the dailies I was surprised at the passenger's panic.

'Hey, watch the road!'

'Hey, tell me about Jansen and the abalone trade. Who's his connection up here?'

'Slow down!'

I eased off the pedal.

We were in open country now, tall trees on the east side, scrub bushes on the ocean side, the water thirty feet down here, there seventy-five rocky cliff steps. 'Jansen?'

'Jansen was a middler.'

*Middler?* 'A fence?'

'Yeah.' Marcus didn't hide his scorn. I had the feeling he'd demoted me a step or two. 'Your brother, the tall kid who looks like you, guess he didn't tell you.'

'He said enough.' Damn Mike. If he'd deigned to tell me . . . But he didn't tell me that, or who knew what else? If he'd . . . 'He said he suspected Jansen had some connection—'

'Suspected! Ha! If he wasn't such a big kid, he never coulda carried the bags of them. Musta been twenty in those bags. Two grand!' He shifted toward me. 'You know the legal limit? Three shells a day! Three!'

'You saw him empty the bag?'

'Nah. I'm not a fool. I didn't poke my head in. But he goes in with the bag; he leaves, a car pulls up, always the same one, black Chevy V-8, Asian guy half his size takes the bag and leaves.'

'So, Grouch, how do you know it was abalone in those bags?'

'What else? You don't make that kind of drop for clams.'

'You're saying you assume, right? You just assume.' I *assumed* Marcus didn't fill his bookcase with Zen books, but still he seemed to catch my meaning.

'I saw the daughters – you remember them?'

'Yeah, Sonja, Maria. Nice kids. Hard workers. Not much English.'

'Enough.'

'Enough for what?'

'Come on,' he said mimicking me. 'Teenage girls, you think they wanted nothing more than to scoop beans? You think they never looked right or left? They saw Jansen strutting around out back. They knew there was more than beans.'

'So?'

'So Jansen controlled everything. What could they do for money? What did they have?'

I held my breath. I didn't want to speculate.

'Shells. One night I saw one of them leave with a big bag, like the abalone bag. She went into a shop that sold tourist stuff – abalone ashtrays. Polished tourist stuff.'

'How much could she make from that?'

'Compared to the nothing Jansen was offering?'

'Point taken. How many shells?'

'A lot. And I'm not just assuming. I could see in the back of the shop when they unloaded twenty-five, thirty shells. A good haul.'

I nodded slowly. Abalone poaching is illegal: that's common knowledge. Transporting illegal abalones is also a crime. But the statute would have run out on both years ago. 'What else, Grouch?'

What had Mike said to me in the park last night? *Change of clothes that meant change of nationality. American shoes. A fast boat drops an hombre before sunset. I get a 'local' to San Fran in time for a late dinner.*

When I'd asked, 'What kind of men?' he'd said, 'Men who could afford to pay.'

'Who did my brother transport to San Francisco, Grouch?'

He went stiff.

I pulled a curve. But the motion of the car had no effect. No vehicle danger could make my passenger any more nervous than he was.

'I brought you up here for a reason, Marcus. Who?'

'Which time?'

# TWENTY-FOUR

'Are you saying my brother transported wanted men, Grouch?'

'Me? Lips sealed.'

'It's a little late for that.'

'Never too late—'

'—for second thoughts?' I laughed. 'That's why they're called second thoughts instead of just thoughts. Because they're a second too late.'

He looked over at me and said nothing. Marcus was on the fence, but odds were he'd come down on the side of stubbornness. He'd dig his feet in and just hope no one would add the rest of his body.

We were coming into a hamlet now – a bar, a general store, gas station and chichi faux rustic restaurant, the kind urban Californians love to discover. Beyond, by the coast and in toward the redwoods, there would be bed-and-breakfasts. The road was straightening, traffic slowing. I was tempted to pull over and lurk in the shadow of a building. But Mike had known this area. I wouldn't blow his cover here, if he was here at all. I eyed Marcus' face in time to see his eyes flicker up and back, as if bouncing a new possibility in his mind.

'Why did you come with me?' I asked as we passed the gas station.

'I don't get out much.'

As annoying as the man had become, I could have believed that. But, of course, I didn't. Was he watching me for someone? Or could he really just be curious about the abalone connection he'd seen all those years ago?

The pavement so far had been relatively smooth, but now it was pocked, split by earth movements, pasted together or not. A sort of macadam sign of 'Nothing important from here on.' To the right, grass led to brush to pines to redwoods all in a hundred yards. To the left was scrub and sea. Ahead, the road squiggled, dipping down into a curve, rising up higher to skim the rocky cliff.

'Where are the abalone?'

Marcus shrugged.

I eased around another curve and back up higher. Afternoon gusts smacked the car, shaking the Martin like it was a VW bug. The windows were shut but the cold air seeped in anyway. I pulled over. 'Get out.'

'What?'

'Out!'

'What the—'

'Help or walk. Your choice.'

Marcus looked through the windshield at the barren coast. I could almost see him gauging how long it would take him to shank it back to the town, in the cold and wind, along the raw edge of the pavement as dusk thickened and drivers sped by. Assuming any did. Assuming they didn't hit him in this place where men don't walk in the dirt beside the road.

'What do you want?'

In Zen we're instructed to 'see life as it is.' I gave Marcus points for doing so and wasting no time. But I didn't fool myself that this moment of realization would last. 'Who was my brother's contact up here?'

'I don't know.'

'Get out!'

'True.'

'What *do* you know?'

The man was sorting, sifting data, like an old-time mainframe hoping spitting out a few perforated cards would convince its keepers to keep it plugged in.

'Who owns the Berkeley house?' I.e., who's behind Mountain Properties?

'The Sorrento place?' The words seemed to escape his mouth before he realized the import.

The rundown house that could be fixed, flipped and sold for close to a million, but was left as is with a ratty basement room available for the needs of one – or more – men who couldn't stay anywhere they might be noticed.

I didn't bother commenting that Marcus knew the place. He didn't try to walk it back.

'Maria.'

Of course! Maria Perez. *Maria.* Marcus, who'd insisted he'd barely spoken to Jansen, much less his wife and daughters who did not speak English, now referred to her by first name.

'Take me to her.'

He shook his head.

A couple back-and-forths later he got her on the phone. The number was in his contacts! 'She'll be here in five. Pull across the street.'

Easier said than done on this sharp curve. But, hey, I'm a professional. To whit I cut a tight circle and pulled up half an inch from the trunk needles of a struggling little star pine that had chosen too windy a cliff spot to survive long. 'You're staying inside.'

He tried to turn his surprise into a shrug. I've seen better.

A black, dirt-sprayed Jeep Cherokee slid in behind us. I waited till the driver got out. 'That her?'

'Who else?'

*You could have called anybody in your contacts list.*

I watched a moment longer, but no one pushed out of the passenger side.

Dusk falls fast at the edge of the continent. Fog sweeps in, turning the setting sun into a fuzzy opaque blush. Blurring faces.

I could just make out her hands. Empty.

I walked toward her. Would I have recognized her, the girl who'd been a teenager when I was twelve? What I recalled from our few hours on the line, me scooping beans, she salsa and guacamole, was her shiny black hair pulled back tight, her face turned down as if salsa were the only important thing in the city. 'You were so focused,' I said.

'It pays to keep your head down.'

*I wouldn't have recognized you.* Her skin was weather-stained and her hair streaked with gray. But the biggest difference was in her eyes. Back then when she did look up they shone with eagerness for the opportunities she hadn't yet imagined. Now they'd seen.

Back then I assumed she knew almost no English. Now she spoke with no trace of an accent.

'Do you remember my brother?'

She let out a big laugh. 'Your big, handsome brother with those yummy blue eyes? My sisters and I, we remembered him a lot. We used to have contests – who could carry their bags of rice fastest, who got the best grade in end-of-the-week test, the winner got him. Then we'd spend the weekend making up stories . . .'

The light was almost gone, so I couldn't be sure she was blushing. Even now I didn't want to hear details. But I wasn't surprised. If there'd been a contest, a race, for attracting girls, Mike would have crossed the finish line before the rest of the boys pushed out of the blocks. I remembered him at Jansen's, moving along the counter before the first 5.00 p.m. customer came in, tossing a comment to Maria as she oiled the grill for the tortillas, flashing a wink at me, pausing just an instant longer before leaning over to whisper to Sonja, then straightening up to give a respectful greeting with just a hint of flirtation for Senora Perez, and if Ynez was in the back, he'd stick his head through the door to say he missed her. All of it focused totally on the receiver; all of it sincere. Why shouldn't they have fallen for him?

'I don't remember you sidling closer to me, hoping I'd tell you if he was a baseball fanatic, what movie he was crazy about, where you could run into him by surprise.' Not the way girls in his school class had.

'We were too busy. Him, he was like the star, you know, on the magazine cover. Far away and all shiny.'

'And yet, Mike was doing the abalone run with you, Maria.'

'You knew about that?'

I'm not sure what I expected but she smiled the same way she had discussing the sisterly contests for him. What did this woman know about me? From Marcus? From the upstairs tenant in her Berkeley dive? It made me nervous, how easily she talked. Was it just the pleasure of reliving the past with one of the few people who had shared it? My urge was to set my feet, ready to take off. But Maria hadn't told me anything she'd kill to conceal. Not so far.

'I didn't know then,' I said. 'He never let on. I didn't find out till now.'

'So long ago. 'nother world back then. It was a game for us, you know? Cloak and dagger. Blanket of risk that wasn't going to smother you.' Her cheeks pooched in a little smile. I remembered that about her.

'Really?'

'Well, you know, we were kids, us girls. We weren't in any real danger and we had no idea how much our parents were. And him . . . he flew above the law.'

'Really?'

'Isn't your brother a cop? Another brother?'

*Was.* 'John? True.'

She shot me a look that encompassed inbred knowledge of nepotism and corruption. Considering the number of times John had pulled Mike out of the fire just before the flames lit his feet, I couldn't disagree.

Considering the times he'd saved *me* . . .

'Everybody liked Mike; no one wanted bad for him.'

I sighed. 'But now, someone's threatening him. It's serious. I need your help.'

Her shoulders tightened under her Polartec shirt. I could see the blue fabric rising toward her neck, pressing in from the sides, as if to squeeze her throat shut. The wind flicked at her short hair. It leapt like tongues of fire. She didn't speak. She probably didn't think she'd moved but I caught her quick glance behind me at Marcus, the shift in expression I couldn't read. 'There's nothing I can—'

'I *need* you. Mike's apartment was almost blown up. This isn't child stuff, Maria.'

She looked more fully over my shoulder, turned and moved away from the car, from Marcus, from the road, making her way between stiff, prickly bushes that can survive the sharp ocean's winds and sun that doesn't break through till late in the day. Runt-of-the-litter plants. They nipped at my pant legs, thorns catching, promising a cluster of tiny holes as I followed her away from the dim light of the open sky above the road, out on to a promontory. A lookout where there was nothing to see.

Near the edge of the cliff she stopped, not bothering to check the stability of the soil beyond, as if to say we weren't going any farther. Waves thundered against the rocky cliff and even up here there was a spray. No chance Marcus was going to hear anything against this roar.

Maria put a hand on my shoulder. 'We were kids then. It was a game. Roll of the dice. You land on *Lose!* and you miss a turn. Worst case, you're out of the game and you have to haul the sodas in from the storage bin. Danger spiced the game but it would go away once we folded up the board and put the dice away. That's what we "knew."'

'As you said.'

'Yes. But listen, this is what I'm saying to you now.' She shifted her weight. 'You know about undertow?'

'Sure.'

'You step in the water. Not deep. Maybe only to your waist. You could walk back to the shore. Or you can keep on walking. And swim. Not to worry; you're sure. And then – no warning – it sucks you down. Smacks you on the bottom so hard all you can think about is your next breath.'

'Yes?'

'And if you struggle, you die. You get what I mean?'

I said nothing, just stood with the icy wind wiping my neck.

'You want to live, you gotta swim with the current. In the current.'

I looked at her, a short, sturdy woman, standing in the wind that she no longer acknowledged. It riffled her hair but her shoulders rose no more. Her hand still on my arm, she took one step closer to the edge, as if tempting the life she'd made her peace with.

'Or, Maria?'

'Or you die.'

'From abalone?'

'Abalone's the gateway of transporting.'

Through my jacket I could feel my shoulder quivering.

'What I'm telling you is we had no choice. My sisters and me, your brother, we were in the undertow before we knew we were in the water. Even moving shell is dangerous. You get caught with illegal abalone, you get squeezed to give up the divers, the runners, the restaurants. Lotta money in shells.'

Something snapped behind me. Breaking scrub branches. I shot a glance back toward the car but nothing had changed.

Maria had spun left so fast I'd barely caught the movement. Her hand, which had been on my shoulder, was now in her pocket. She waited, eyes alert, body ready to run. Or pounce?

She inhaled and exhaled slowly then said, 'People hock their lives for restaurants. Fish and Game shuts them down, they lose it all; owe it all. You see?'

'I do. But still, you were kids.'

She hesitated. 'You would be better off not knowing this. Your brother, he didn't know till too late. I don't know which way Rico reeled him in—'

'Rico?'

'His contact here. Dead. Long time ago.' She stopped, stared directly at me. 'Shot and shot and shot. His face was mush.'

'In the city?'

'On Valencia.'

'But Mike wasn't involved in that!' The words fell out of my mouth. *Please make him* not *have been caught up in shooting someone!*

'No, no.' She seemed shocked, too, and I found that comforting.

'Maria, tell me how my brother got involved. I need to know.' *Please make it not his fault!*

She nodded slowly, as if understanding a sister's need. 'I don't know about Mike but this is how it went down most times. Driver gets here. Rico says there was no diving today. Or maybe he sent the shells with someone else. He feels bad about the kid wasting his day, spending all that on gas for nothing. But, listen, this guy needs a lift into the city. He can make it worth your while.'

Her hand was back on my shoulder and she pulled me in a bit closer. 'Most times that worked. But some kids – Mike maybe – were suspicious. For them the story was the illegal was a refugee from a camp high up in the interior, a place where he was tortured. That he had to get to his people in the city. He could pay, he'd stolen money when he escaped; was going to use it for food, to keep him safe. But he would give it to the driver.' She was breathing as heavily as the wind. 'Mike, what could he do?

'Look out there.' She turned toward the sea, taking a step

closer. Her hand tightened on my shoulder. 'Look down. This was one of the entry spots.'

There was just enough light to see the crash, the spray.

'Forty-six feet down. You need a rope and someone you can trust at the top. This place, Fish and Game, ICE, no one watches here. It's too hard to climb out. Rope breaks, nothing to hold; you fall, you crack your skull open like a clam.

'The only men who are delivered here are the ones with bounties that would keep you for a lifetime. For them every other spot is too dangerous. You get what I'm saying?'

I didn't answer.

'Let me just tell you this. Mike drove Santino, one of the "refugees," to San Francisco. The next week the guy went at it with some locals, killed two of them and a local couple in the crossfire.' She swallowed. 'Those shots changed our lives. The first thursday in April. By the end of the week we were gone. Every year on the anniversary—'

'Two days ago!'

She nodded.

'But Mike? Did he know about Santino?'

'When he drove him to the city? No. He may have suspected the man he drove had a price on his head. May have guessed he was in drugs. But he didn't know he was Santino, the most feared *sicario*—'

'*Sicario?* Hitman?'

'What you might call the supervisor of all the hitmen in the cartel. Santino . . . he had a lot of blood on his hands.'

'But Mike didn't know that back then?' It was almost a prayer.

'Maybe no. Probably no. But me and my family, when we heard about it, we knew who he was. I told Mike. And Santino, he knew we knew.'

'Which is why you disappeared?' I asked, though I knew that wasn't true.

'I thought,' she said, 'when Mike went missing that he'd escaped. When he stayed missing all those years, I wondered, did Santino get him? Was he dead? I lit a candle for him, but I don't put much faith in that.

'I'll tell you, when I heard that he was back, I was surprised. Amazed.'

I nodded slowly.

'And then I lit another candle. But like I say, I don't put much stock in wax.'

'And yet, here you are.'

'Me telling you this, it's what the candle gets you.'

'What should I do?'

'Walk away. Don't look behind you.'

'And Mike? What should I do for him?'

'Pray.'

At the far edge of the ocean, the red ball of sun bounced and sunk as if sucked under. A minute ago we had stood in the dim light and shadows, now the world was just dark. To my right I could make out branches against a slightly less dark sky, to my left the slight sparkle of the water far below. The wind backed off, its dusk work over. Suddenly the waves crashed louder against the rocky cliff.

'Pray? I'd have been better off lighting a candle. At least there'd be light.' I thought Maria might laugh but she didn't. Now, in the dark, I couldn't make out her expression at all. But I hadn't come all this way to leave empty. The road forked here, question-wise. Like our options leaving this spot. I opted for the verbal path back through the scrub toward the street. 'Maria, I wondered . . . You and Mike?'

'Oh no.'

'Really? I watched him. He had a word for everyone, but for you it was more, a longer look, a comment only you laughed at. There was that time he followed you into the back and I thought he was going to kiss you until your father—'

She sighed – regret? Or just reminiscence? 'Poppa thought the same. I paid for that, believe me.'

'But Mike, would he have kissed you?' *Did he? Then? Later?*

She didn't answer. If I had been able to see her reaction . . . Had her hand tightened on my shoulder?

'Maria, this is the time he needs you. We have to find out who's trying to kill him before . . . they do. Please!'

Her hand did tighten now. We were five feet from the cliff edge. It would be so easy for her to toss me over.

She might be *thinking* she could throw me over. I could have told her: not likely. But I kept that to myself.

And there was Marcus sitting warm in the Martin. She might be remembering that he knew we were here. A complication.

Or he could be sitting there waiting for her to finish me off.

'We're here at the edge of the world. No one knows. No one can hear you. I won't implicate you. I just want to save my brother!'

Now it was my shoulder shaking against her hand. The wind snapped sharp dry leaves against each other. It iced my neck, my hands I didn't dare put in my pockets.

'A name. Just tell me a name. Then go and you won't hear from me again. You'll know you saved him, that he's OK. Just look in the *Chronicle*; we'll get a mention of him there. It won't involve you, but you'll know you made it possible. Just a name!'

She glanced toward the water.

I went with the other fork in the verbal road. The question that would set the way things were between us.

# TWENTY-FIVE

I slapped Maria's hand off my shoulder. 'Here you are. Safe. And you own the house in Berkeley. With the basement you keep for people where no one will find them.'

She shifted. Like she was setting her feet. In the dark I couldn't be sure. I could hear her breathe now, but she didn't speak.

'This transport scheme, you're the one who came out smelling like roses. House in Berkeley? What'd it sell for? Eight hundred, nine hundred thousand dollars? Clear? It's not like you'd've been putting up paper for a loan, right? Collateral in kilos? Not like Santino would. He paid cash, right? And put it in your name, Mountain Properties.'

Again I waited, but she still didn't speak.

'You were the innocent girl. What did you say about you and Mike? You were in before you realized it? No escape. But you're safe here. So how is that, Maria? Where is Santino?'

She shifted.

'Or Maria, is there a Santino at all? Or is it just you? Was it just you all along?'

'I was a kid!'

'You're not a kid now. Your family vanished; Santino isn't in sight. You're the one with the safe house.'

'Vanished isn't dead.'

'Vanished can be tracked down. I found Mike. No one tracked down your family because no one cared. But now, if they're connected to Santino, to the killings that took out innocent civilians . . . Believe it, they can be found.'

She said nothing. Didn't move. Barely breathed.

It had all been theoretical until now. Neither of us truly the target. I stepped in. 'I can make it happen. Police, feds, ICE scrambling to see who closes in first. Your choice.' The wind, cold, sharp with brine, cut through me. One shove into the sea and she could solve her problem.

Time stopped.

After an eternity, she spoke. Her voice cut through the wind. It seemed to echo. 'What do you want from me?'

'Take me to Santino.'

She stood frozen, her black form outlined by the black sky and the pale glimmer off the ocean. 'Do you want to die?'

'Take me to him. Now!'

'You don't have any idea what you're asking.' She sighed. 'Wait. I'll bring him to you. Wait here.'

'At the edge of the cliff? I don't think so.'

She threw up her hands. 'I'm putting my life on the line for you, Darcy. I can't take you to Santino. You know why? I don't know where he stays. All these years, I don't know. That's how he stays alive. I call. I leave a number. He calls back.'

It was this or come up empty. 'Fine. Do it.'

I'd wondered if there'd be cell coverage out here, but, at least for Maria, it was no problem.

She punched in a number. 'Maria,' she said, and clicked off.

I had liked Maria. She'd done me small favors without the promise of return. Lent me a cloth to tie my hair back on the food line when I forgot. Showed me the 'nibble bowl' in the back where you could scoop a mouthful of abalone mix in a piece of tortilla on the way to the bathroom and be back on the line before anyone noticed. Little things. She hadn't pumped me about Mike. She'd cared when he went missing.

But trust? Like my brother John says: When it's your neck or hers, trust goes out the window.

She moved back from the edge of the cliff and we stood where the scrub brush broke the dirt. The wind didn't get us here. It seemed, for a moment, silent.

'Maria,' I said, to get her attention. 'How is it Grouch knew how to find you?'

'I gave him my number.'

'But why? Careful as you are, why leave a path to you?'

'It's a number. Nothing more. Did you think I live here? You think we're meeting in my backyard?'

'Not likely,' I said, though that wasn't entirely the truth. But I wasn't about to admit that.

'Why Marcus?'

'He keeps an eye on the old place. Someone comes nosing around, he calls.'

She had started walking toward the road.

'Have people? Other than me?'

'Enough.'

'Who?'

I didn't expect a reply; didn't get one. 'Is it just guys trying to get a bead on Santino? Or trying to get to you?'

She turned toward me. 'Don't you get it? It's the same thing. No one wants me unless they're after him. I'm the message number, that's all.'

'But is it just his business associates?' I said, for lack of a better term. 'Or others? Reporters? Police?'

'Use to be. Early on. Cops. Private cops. Reporters digging into the dead. Nosy old men who'd managed to get the number. Was there a link, those two civilians? Or were they just collateral damage?'

'Were they?'

'Yeah. Wrong place. No connection. Santino told me. He hated shooting bystanders.'

'Really?'

'It's messy. Causes problems. Cops don't care if you shoot your own, but they come after you for taking out locals.'

'You believed Santino?'

'On that.'

*Nosy old men.* 'Does the name Wally Ellis mean anything to you?'

'I don't remember names. I've trained myself not to.'

We were almost to the road when her phone rang. She put it to her ear, didn't speak. Clicked off. To me she said, 'We'll take your car.'

'How far?'

'Not far.'

'Where?'

'Just drive. I'll tell you when to stop.'

Was the deck stacked in her favor as much as she imagined? She might know I was a stunt double, but there was no way she could have realized how many car gags I'd done. With me driving, some of those cards were migrating to my side of the table.

The tree cover gave way to sky. For an instant the blacktop shone bright as noon. The Martin almost glowed, its black paint so highly buffed. I pulled open the driver's door.

The car was empty.

'Marcus isn't here. Where—'

'Don't worry about him.'

*Don't worry about him.* Not what you say about an old guy who wandered off to take a leak.

*Don't worry about him.* Fat chance! I shot a 360. No sign of him. Don't worry when a man disappears in the outback? When he might have been picked up by someone who will be following you? Or waiting for you? Don't worry!

*What is the price of rice in Luling?* No point in speculating when you can't know the answer.

I got in the car and started the engine, thinking of the major Zen instruction: *Be aware.* I checked the rearview, both side mirrors and the rearview one last time and pulled onto the road.

My phone rang.

'Ignore it.'

Her voice was tighter than it had been on the cliff. I glanced over. Her head was moving slightly side to side.

Danger wasn't going to come from the phone. I let it go to message. I was just pleased it was finally getting reception.

I'd driven here in daylight but now, in the dark, the headlights seemed like small white spots on the macadam, turning the night around them blacker. Curves erupted out of nowhere. On the way up I'd hit the gas to catch the centripetal force. Now I braked abruptly when the road veered right or left into nothing, like a driver who'd never seen a mountain road.

The road curved out along the edge of a promontory, well out into the ocean. I'd noticed it coming up but hadn't paid much attention. Now I was alert for turnouts, places Santino could be hiding, spots that I might need if I had to make a fast three point and run. But the promontory was so long and narrow, the road was like a line drawn around a forefinger with a pen. If someone had cut a path through at the knuckle, that would have saved us a quarter of an hour.

My phone rang again. Automatically I reached.

'Give it to me.'

'I'll let it go to message.'

'No, let me check the caller.'

'How could he have my number?'

She just stuck out her hand.

I gave.

A minute passed as the car dipped and hit a rise along the cliff. I remembered Marcus hanging onto the door for that one.

Maria held out the phone. 'They'll keep,' she said. 'I turned it off.'

*Be aware.*

'Can you move this car faster?'

'This from a woman in the death seat?'

'He doesn't like to wait.'

*Well, who does?* But I sped up on the straightaway and stared harder, as if that would show me any danger a second sooner. If there'd been houses, or the wonder of streetlights . . . Even reflectors at the curves would give strangers a fighting chance. But all the odds were with the locals here. Like driving around San Francisco trying to find an entrance to the Bay Bridge in the city, as my sister Janice complained every time she drove in.

'Here. Pull over.'

'Where? There's nothing but bushes.'

'Stop!'

She had the door open before I'd braked. 'Stay here. I'll be back in a minute.' She edged out, but still I could hear branches scraping Gary's expensive paint job. 'You can check those messages of yours while I'm gone.'

Like I wouldn't!

# TWENTY-SIX

It's not easy to check messages while eyeing the rearview, the side mirrors and keeping ears pricked for footsteps.

From Janice: 'I'm at the BART station. I'll . . . oooh, there's the train.'

Janice: 'I'm in the city. You know, Darcy, this underground switching system is so confusing. It used to be you just stood on Market Street and watched for the streetcar. Now you have to figure out which level to go to. Yeah, I know I'm in the left side. Sorry, Darce, that was some guy. Ooh, there's the N-car.'

Janice: 'I got off at Cole and Carl like the map said, but I can't tell where I am. I can't even see the park from here. The last time I was in the Haight it sure didn't look like this. It's like the place got a whole new wardrobe. Excuse me! Excuse me, can you point me toward the park?'

Janice: 'Where did you say Mike's car was? Oh, never mind, there . . .'

Gracie: 'Hi. Listen, have you heard from Janice? She was supposed to be here. We're going to that Burmese place at Fourth and Clement, the one with that great salad. Yeah, I know Janice isn't time-reliable, but I had to make a reservation and if we lose it, we'll be eating at midnight. Call me.'

Gary: 'Darce, Gracie just called me. She's worried about Janice. I said I'd drive over and have a look. Where did you park my car? Call me.'

Gary: 'Seriously, call me. I can't find the car anywhere. Jeez, I just hope it hasn't been boosted, stripped, headed for the border. Jeez. Are you using it? It's OK if you are. Just let me know.'

John: 'What the hell's going on? Where are you? Did you take Gary's Aston Martin? Do you know what that car's worth? You scrape it and you could get your face lifted for less than the rehab. Call me, I'll catch a ride and drive it back.'

John: 'And where the hell is Mike? Why can't he pick up his own car? And what . . . Sheesh, this family!'

Heather: 'Darcy? You said to call you if we saw anything unusual. And, well, your car blew up. I mean, right across the street.' It sounded like she was swallowing. I could hear clanging and sirens in the background and voices. 'The police came and an ambulance. They took the driver out on a stretcher. The driver . . . I hate to say this, but do you think it was supposed to be you? Be careful.'

There were three more messages. My hand was shaking over the phone. I wanted to stay in this moment, in the safety of not knowing what I'd know in a minute. What I ninety percent knew now and couldn't bear to believe.

Mom: 'Darcy, honey, there's been an explosion in the Haight. White car. Woman taken to the hospital. I've got to go. I . . . I just didn't want you to hear this on the radio. Call me when you can.'

Leo: 'Darcy, your sister Janice is in San Francisco General. She's got burns on her legs and arms. They don't know how bad it is. She was in the white Honda; there was an explosion. Your family's all at the hospital. I'm heading there. Renzo's driving me.

'Darcy, where are you? Call me and let me know you're all right before your family starts to wonder about you.'

Before, he meant, they were huddled in the waiting room, frantic for word on Janice, each of them working their sources, each of them being told it was too soon to know anything. Then their attention would turn to me. There'd be speculation on my whereabouts, why I hadn't notified anyone I was leaving the city. And, though Leo wouldn't know this yet, there'd be Gary wondering about his car.

*I asked Janice to get the car.*

*She wouldn't have been there, but for me.*

*Wouldn't be in SF General, in the trauma unit, but for me.*

*Wouldn't be – No! – maybe dying.*

*Because of me.*

*Because of Mike.*

*And me.*

I just sat, suddenly aware of the icy air around me, the wind battering the windows. The dark dark.

I checked the last message.

John: 'Just picked up your call.' No recriminations, tone so deadened I wouldn't have recognized his voice. He hadn't even bothered to tell me to call him. That scared me more than all the other messages.

I clicked on Leo's number and hit reply.

Nothing.

Damn. Leo would have given me facts without fuss. He'd tell me not to get caught in emotion. To acknowledge the guilt, the drenching fears without naming them, to not traipse along those mushy threads of thought. To just do the next thing.

I did the next thing. I called back Mom.

Nothing.

Shit! Was I out of range? How could that be? Maria had coverage up here. Why didn't I? If I'd shelled out for a better plan . . . No. She had a need for it; I hadn't expected to.

Now, for the first time, I looked at the time of those messages. Three hours ago. I was still on the coast road then. In and out of range, probably.

Three hours ago. Janice had been in the hospital for three hours. I could get an update from patient services. I could—

Out of range.

Three hours. She could be dying while I sat up here.

I turned on the engine.

*Do the next thing.*

I checked the mirrors.

*Do the next thing.*

I reached for the brake, but I knew as I did it that it was not the next thing. It was just a thing. The next thing was . . .? I could feel the *dokusan* room, Garson-roshi and me sitting cross-legged on zafus, the candle burning on the altar beside him, whiffs of incense floating in the air. Him saying, 'What is the next thing? You know.'

Time was passing, I was desperate to be on the road. I . . .

*I . . .*

I was not essential to Janice now. In the flock of siblings, I might not even make the cut into her room. And she'd have Mom. My being with her was essential only to me.

I took a breath, sat in the silence, listening through the silence to the sounds in it, the wind, not steady but erratic like a volley of tennis balls hit by dozens of racquets. Trees snapping branches into each other. Leaves brushing, crackling.

I listened for what I didn't hear – Maria and Santino pushing through the brush, hurrying back to my car.

Then I did the next thing.

# TWENTY-SEVEN

I'd been worried when Maria got out, that she'd scrape the paint. *Scrape the paint! Janice might be dying.*

Lights out, I eased the car on the narrow road. The shoulder was the width of the car. I backed up against the brush, eased out, backed again, and on to the shoulder facing north. Santino had to be parked back along this road.

Where were they? Maria had been gone a long time. I had no real sense how long. Long enough for the world to change for the worse.

Had she just left me? Hooked up with Santino, walked down some path to his vehicle and driven off? Why not?

Or not even called Santino. Called someone. Some number. Talked to air. Walked down a path to somewhere? Called a friend and was on her way home?

Could she—

And what about Marcus? Why had he gotten out of the warm, safe car where I'd left him? To check on me? More likely to spy on Maria and me. To spy for Santino? Even more likely to take a leak. Was he trotting grouchily south along the side of that long finger of road? I could picture him, his too long brown hair blowing around like field grass, him swiping it uselessly out of his eyes and wrapping his red and black striped scarf tighter around his neck. He'd have tried calling Maria, and stomped on, cursing the lack of cell phone coverage.

I peered into the darkness, prepared to see his stubby figure trudging around the fingernail of the road and down toward me, panting. And all the while blaming me.

I rounded the nail and headed up the side of the finger, trying to figure how far it was to the place I'd left him. The road was so close to the edge there was barely room to pull over, much less make a turn. So I noticed the spot, slowed, squinting to see Marcus.

Which is how come I saw the truck at all.

The lights were off. I almost missed it pulling out a hundred yards away. Just a flash of taillights, engine not loud enough to drown out the wind. Driven with the bravado of one who knew the land, the roads, who had all the advantages.

Not likely! Stunt driver in an Aston Martin; no way that truck could lose me.

Gunshots aside.

I slowed till a curve separated us and cut my lights. Ahead the taillights flashed again. The truck was slowing, not as if it was about to turn, but enough to allow the driver to maneuver the familiar road in the dark. Even so he kept hitting the brakes. I kept following the taillights.

When the road rounded the next promontory and the land was briefly between us, I switched on my high beams, wide-viewed my gaze to take in the terrain, and to plant that picture over the blackness when I switched off the lights. I'd learned the trick early on doing a balance gag blind. See the ground and you're fine. Close your eyes and you wobble. If you're very good you hold position a minute, ninety seconds, before you flail like a 'copter with engine fail and crash. But keep the picture of the ground in your mind when your eyes are closed and you can last four or five minutes, which is plenty long enough for any director.

The road was leveling off; my wheels would catch a curve in a few feet. No shoulder. Curve sharp right. I inhaled as if to pull the terrain in through my pores, then switched off the lights.

The world was dead black. I couldn't see the speedometer but I had to be doing double the sensible speed. Everything in my body screamed, Brake! At least slow down.

I felt the pull of the curve, stepped on the gas and rode it to the right. The picture in my mind didn't go as far as around the corner. I squinted against the dark for the darker line that would be the trees and scrub, and let the engine slow. Ahead, taillights flashed. I shot a beam to them, like a surveyor, and hit the gas. The road sank fast. Like driving into a sock. If I hit the turn too late, I'd slam into the inner cliff wall. And bounce back and roll over the far edge down the rocky cliff into the sea. I wouldn't have to worry about the car floating; I'd be dead by then.

I slowed.

The taillights came on ahead, so much higher they were like

airplane lights. They stayed on. Good sign. The driver had been taking no chances on me following them, but now felt safe enough to use headlights.

I kept the gas steady – no telltale engine roar – and counted on the snapping of the trees to cover that sound. I was gaining, coming close enough to make out the bed in the back. A pickup. Not new. It was almost abreast a right-hand curve. I took a chance – drivers don't look behind when they're maneuvering a curve – hit the gas, and came within fifty feet of the bumper as he made the turn.

The truck was old, the seat a bench. No passenger. Driver only.

Who? Maria? Santino?

The truck veered into the high right-hand curve. The inside wall – dirt, sand, brush – curtained it. It could turn off any moment. I had to make a move.

I turned on the high beams. The sudden bright blinded me.

I didn't see the sheriff's car until it swung the curve and barely missed me as it sped down past me on the ocean side of the road. In the rearview I could see its flashers, suddenly on.

I slowed. A lot.

More flashers were coming at me. It rounded a curve, flashers going like Christmas. I doused the lights and pulled far right, right wheels off the pavement.

Boxy truck. Was it medics? Behind me now the sirens cut the wind.

Ahead was just the memory of lights. No new flashers.

No pickup truck.

I waited.

Fat lot of good.

The sheriff could be hightailing it to a citizen having a heart attack. To a woman who'd run out of gas. A boy who'd hit a tree. To a hot poker game in town. To any call he could get on his phone with greater range.

The pickup was gone. I spotted the skinniest of turnouts, cut sharp and followed the flashers.

# TWENTY-EIGHT

The sheriff's lights were still flashing, their cars pointed west toward the cliff. I pulled up by the struggling little star pine, where I'd sat with Grouch Marcus an hour ago, waiting for Maria to arrive. Now medics ran parallel to the road, ready to roll fast. Civilian vehicles bookended them. Impressive how fast the locals had caught the call. I slid up in front, ready to shoot onto the hardtop and head south.

'What's going on?' I asked a young, blond guy, dressed like L.L.Bean meets 1970.

'Floater.'

'Someone's dead down there, over the cliff?' I said.

'Yeah. Like I said, floater.'

'Man? Woman?'

'No word. They haven't hooked the body out.'

I started toward the cliff. He caught my arm. 'Roped off.'

'There's no crime-scene tape.'

'That's me.'

'Human crime-scene tape?' Maybe he was a civilian volunteer. Whatever. I wasn't likely to get past. Not in a direct line. I pulled my inadequate cotton vest tighter around me and said, 'So what do you guys think happened?'

'Coulda been anything. Idiot walking in the dark. Tourist decides to make a call. Drops his phone, leans over to grab it. Kersplatt.'

I shivered. It was all too likely an explanation. Except that Maria or Santino would know better. Even Mike . . . 'Any signs of a struggle?'

'Edge of the cliff, there's always a struggle. No one just trots over.'

Point taken.

I wished I could call John, ask him to pull strings, find some buddy who had a friend who knew a deputy up here.

Truth was, if I had been able to call John I wouldn't have finished a sentence before he was haranguing me about 'scenes of suspicion.' *Jesus, Darcy, don't you remember anything? In a scene of suspicion when they start looking for perpetrators, the first one they grab is the stranger. Walk away. Get back in the car. Jesus, Darcy, are you driving Gary's big-time lawyer car? Could you tempt these guys more? Get out of there. Just move. Jesus, Darcy!*

Wise words, if not spoken as Father Murphy would have liked.

A pickup slammed to a stop in front of the Aston. There was still time for me to ease out of here. Two boys and a girl jumped out. 'Hey, Jed, whadaya got?'

'Floater,' the blond, Jed, said.

'Diver?'

'Nah. In cloth.'

'Isn't it late for divers?' I asked.

The four of them laughed. 'Never too late to die in your wet suit,' Jed said. 'But this body isn't in rubber. This floater didn't get his hose caught thirty feet down and float up to the surface an hour later. This one fell.'

'Or jumped?'

'You're not from here, are you?' one of the truck boys asked.

I could hear John in my head. *Jeez, Darcy, that's right, throw off your cloak of safety.* 'I don't know this spot,' I said, hoping that would blur my status.

'Cliff here juts out like ten feet down. You jump, you get yourself hooked.'

'Hey, you know what "off the hook" is from?' the girl put in. 'From the old Mafia, like in the movies when they hung a stoolie on a meat hook. Off the hook, get it?'

They hooted. Even Jed, wavering between his official role and his adolescence.

'So,' I said, 'does that mean he or—' god forbid – 'she was pushed?'

'Guess so. Wow, that's so creepy.'

'Man? Woman? What do you think?'

'Man, sure?'

'A broad could take out another broad,' one of the boys declared.

Could Maria shove Santino over the edge? If he didn't see it coming? But of course these kids couldn't know. And, really, neither did I. Had Marcus described Santino at all? No. I was dead sure of that. He probably assumed everyone who knew about Santino could recognize him. And if you couldn't, then you had no business trying to get a picture of him. Old enough to have been smuggled ashore two decades ago, that was all Marcus had said. A man who could have been living here, intent on assimilating for twenty years; a man smart enough to be the supervisor of hitmen in a drug ring and know when to walk away; a man who had shot four people – four that we knew of – in San Francisco and had never been arrested. He must be a master of fitting in. He could have shoved Maria over the cliff and slipped into the crowd. Among his friends in the crowd. His long-term friends. The ones who'd moved up here in the last decade probably thought of him as Charlie, the old guy who raises sheepdogs or watches birds.

Was he big enough, strong enough to push Maria over the cliff? Or Mike? Mike who I did not know was anywhere near here!

'You want a brew?' one of the boys was asking.

*When hiding out in a crowd, scope out the pecking order. Don't separate a couple; connect with the single.* That from Mike. I scoped, sidled up next to the speaker, a tall, thin guy with dark shoulder-length hair as curly as my own.

*Don't be pushy; let him bring you in.*

'Yeah. You got any food?'

'Nah. Should I make a run?' He looked at Jed, who said, 'You got time.'

I stepped back and waited to see if anyone was eager to go with him. No takers. *The single!* I copped a ride.

'Darcy,' I said.

'Ephraim. Hi Dotty.'

At the Gas 'n' Gobble, I used the Hen's, bought the biggest cling-wrapped sandwich on the counter, a Coke and a bottle of water. I could have downed the entire po' boy on the ride back but I made myself wait. *Eating is good cover.* That from Mike. *Don't talk; listen, then agree. Nothing like agreement to make yourself fit in.*

We pulled up at the scene, so close to the interior cliff wall I had to squeeze under the wheel to get out. The only thing that had changed was the temperature. Probably wasn't ten degrees colder but it felt like it. I'd left the city in the afternoon wearing a T-shirt and a vest. This was wool country.

*They'll help you to fit in.*

'Cold,' I muttered.

'I got a blanket in the bed. You don't mind dog hair.'

'Hardly. I've got a dog of my own.' I swallowed hard. Duffy! Only his innate pickiness and Mom's devotion to spoiling him with her beef stew had saved him from the poison.

Ephraim's dog was white. One who could have used a bath. I wrapped the blanket around me and was grateful. Doubly so when Ephraim's friends assured him nothing had happened.

'Floater,' Jed said.

'Huh?' I prodded, biting off a corner of sandwich. It was all bread, but that was just fine.

'Drowner, they pull out all stops to get him out, do CPR or whatever. Keep him alive. Floater's already dead. No rush—'

'You can say that again,' a guy groaned.

'No rush because now, see, the focus is on preserving evidence. Body's evidence, see. Coroner's not going to be happy if it's full of hook marks. Especially in a case like this.'

'Like this?' I took another bite. The corner of a thin slice of ham had made it into it.

'Questionable cause of death. Sheriff's got to see the body; then the coroner's got to examine it, you know, saws and baggies.'

'Yuck.'

'That's the protocol.' Jed glanced around the group like a visiting professor.

'Hey, are we going to be hanging here all night while the sheriff checks him out down there by the water?'

'You might think so—' he really was into the visiting prof. bit – 'but tonight, no. It's too exposed down there. Nowhere to lay the floater out. No decent light.'

I could have asked how carefully the sheriff would move the body, but I knew the answer: very. So I ate. And waited. Ate, and nudged the talk back into the beginning of the speculations.

*Don't underestimate how often a group people can say the same thing. Larger the group, greater the times.*

Mike had kept himself unnoticed for twenty years. I knew he had to have been good at it, but I hadn't quite realized what a study he'd made. By now he could be a visiting professor himself. I found myself looking around at the edges of the group to spot him fitting in.

When the deputies finally hoisted the body up, not in a bag, but on a stretcher, it was well after midnight. Two on each side, like pallbearers they hoisted it up over the edge, shifted their feet and moved slowly toward the road.

Our group moved closer. A larger bunch shifted in from the other side.

'Hey, get back!' the sheriff yelled. 'Get the doors open.'

'I thought they were going to examine here!'

'Guess not.'

I pushed forward, between the taller wool-clad bodies. But the deputies' torsos blocked the corpse's head and hips. A blanket covered the body from the neck down.

*Head free; no chance of outside fibers.* That had been from John.

The doors to the medical van swung open. The deputies carrying hips to feet, shifted to get purchase and hoist the stretcher in.

*Without me seeing the body!*

*If there's a problem, spread the guilt.* Lott family dictum.

I grabbed handfuls of the dog's blanket, braced and shoved the men on either side of me. Ephraim stumbled into a woman in front. The other guy hit the ground. 'Goddamn it!' 'What the fuck!'

I raced forward, looked at the dead face.

Not Mike!

Hands grabbed my shoulders. I shook free, stared at the face again, and gasped.

The hands grabbed again. I let myself be shoved back into the crowd; dropped to the ground and held my ankle as if I'd been one of the injured.

As men and a woman pushed themselves up, I abandoned the blanket, joined the grumble of the slightly injured, moved back and forth 'walking it off.' And when the official party pulled off in a firework of flashers, I sidled to the Aston, turned on the lights and headed south.

In the town I stopped for gas, for the bathroom again, grabbed a cup of coffee and a Snickers bar and was back in the car in five minutes. I tried the phone. Nothing.

I tried again. As if the power of my need to know about Janice would fuel the phone lines.

I downed the chocolate and coffee before I had time to decry the latter and left. Fast as I intended to take these curves, I was going to need both hands.

# TWENTY-NINE

I was still shaking from seeing the body under that blanket.

I was still desperate to know if my sister was on life support, even alive.

I wanted to call, to at least try again, but common sense told me that would only slow me up. So I drove.

The road which I'd used to intimidate Marcus in the afternoon hadn't changed, except now it was dark and I was driving not on the inner – hill – side of the road but on the ocean side, my wheels feet from the edge of the hardtop, the shoulder fading into the dark, the rocks jutting from the shore below. *Slow down!* one of those reflective signs shouted. *Tight curve ahead. 15 mph max!*

I swore, but I slowed, creeping, like trudging through caramel, around curve after endless curve.

Finally, gratefully, the sign for the road inland to the freeway appeared. I tried the phone. Nothing, still.

Then I turned and drove in among the trees.

I have a bad history with trees. A fear from childhood. It's been humiliating, especially in my line of work. But now I barely noticed the darker trunks, the waving branches against the slightly less black all around. I shifted from the high beams, on in case of animals, to the standards on the straight-aways. I took curves too fast now, grateful for this very good car, not letting myself consider how bad a crash would be here in the middle of nowhere.

And when the horizon bleached from black to gray – from lights, not sun – I could have cheered. The freeway this far north isn't crowded in the early morning, but flickers of headlights heading north, thin streams of taillights going south to San Francisco were like sunshine.

I veered on to the freeway south and sighed. For a city kid, hitting a wide straightway is like coming home. It's like seeing sidewalk after miles of scrub brush, or lawns that slope down to a street with no accommodation for walkers. Like seeing doors that open to stores instead of close to strangers.

Now there would be cell coverage. I could find out about Janice.

Now it was 2.30 in the morning. Friday.

Who did I want to chance dragging out of bed after a long, fearful day?

Assuming they were not still at the hospital. Or worse.

I was stalling. I could have called Gracie, but not without getting more medical detail and survey of possible turns for the catastrophic worse than I wanted to know right now – or ever. Gary would give me a straighter answer, but then there'd be discussion of the state of the car.

I realized with a start, the right person to call in a pressure situation would be Janice. When I was stranded down the inland freeway, almost to LA, she was the one I called. Odd, she was my least-close sibling, the one who'd exiled herself to the East Bay. She'd give me the facts without a layer of blame.

No way was I going to wake Mom if she'd gotten herself to sleep.

Which left John. And I sure wasn't dealing with him in the middle of the night. Not when I was speeding down the freeway, having left a crime scene without letting on what I knew about the victim. And talking on the phone.

As much as it galled me, I pulled over to get Heather's number and hit 'reply.'

'Darcy?'

'How's Janice?' I said without intro.

There was a moment of silence during which I realized Heather would have no idea what I was talking about. 'Janice,' I said, 'my sister in the hospital. My sister who was in the car!'

'It was awful! The bang just about split my eardrums. The smoke, you'd of thought it was a forest fire. Boots got his hands burned trying to get her out of the driver's seat. He's got these big mitts of bandages on both hands. He can't pick up anything—'

'But how's Janice?'

'Ambulance took forever to arrive. The medics kind of tossed her into the back of their van, you know, like she was a duffle in an airporter. Then it sped away down those bumpy streets.

You know, the city could spend some money fixing the streets. I thought my head would hit the roof—'

'You rode in the ambulance with her?'

'Yeah. Boots just needed someone to deal with his hands—'

'Did Tom do that?'

'Tom?' It was a moment before she said, 'Oh, him. He split after the cops turned him loose. You know, after he went back into Wally's place for his notes. Cops kept him for hours, freaked him out. He said if they wanted to question him more they could haul themselves to Pittsburgh. He was long gone before they put Janice in the ambulance. Poor Janice, she was moaning. Screaming some. Like the pain was unbearable.'

'Omigod!'

'You should have heard her. The medics had given her a shot, but it must not have taken. Or maybe the pain was just too awful.'

'Omigod. Oh . . .'

'Oh, Darcy, you must feel terrible.'

'Yeah.'

'Really terrible.'

'How is she now? Where is she?'

'It took forever to get across town and then there was a back-up in the burn unit. Maybe if they'd gotten to her sooner . . . but you never know, right?'

'Heather! It was great of you to stay with Janice—'

'No problem. I've had crises – deaths – in my family. I know what this is like. Other people don't understand, but I know the suffering. So I was—'

'How . . . is . . . she . . . now?' *Dammit!*

'Still in the hospital, but stable.'

'Who's with her?'

'Besides me?'

'You're still there?'

'Someone had to stay. No one contacted your family for hours. Janice was crying out for you all, but no one came. No one was here but me. I told her I was your friend, your close friend, so at least she'd think she had someone.'

*The hospital didn't call? Didn't Janice have any contact info in her wallet?* Possibly no, I thought. There'd been a long time; the family weren't the ones she'd call first. *Sheesh Heather, couldn't you have called us?* But, of course, she had called me. And I had been out of range. My hand was shaking on the phone. I had to swallow hard before I could say, 'Who else is there now?'

She listed off the full complement of siblings, and Mom.

'Thanks, Heather. This was above and beyond of you. Where are you headed now? To the airport? Going home? Your event must be over.'

'We're staying at your mother's. Boots can't leave for at least a day. Obviously we can't stay where we were – in the crime scene. So your Mom said, "Come." She said there were plenty of extra rooms. I'm taking Boots there now. Your Mom said there'd be beef stew in the fridge, that we should help ourselves. I guess that means I'll be helping Boots . . . because of his bandages. Though he's way better off than Janice.'

'Thanks, again.' I clicked off. Now I called Mom.

'Darcy, honey, where are you?'

'Good question. Somewhere north of Santa Rosa. Tell Gary I've got his car. How's Janice?'

'Sedated. But she'll be fine.'

'Really? I just talked to Heather—'

Mom laughed.

'The mother of a woman in the burn unit is laughing?'

That made her laugh harder. When she pulled herself together, she said, 'That Heather is something of a sad sack, don't you think?'

I hadn't thought about that before tonight but it was hard to disagree. 'What about the burns?'

'She's got some on her legs. Fourth degree. Or is it first? Whichever's least. It'll probably scar, but you know Janice, she's never been one to flash her flesh around. Plus, she was wearing corduroy pants so thick she could have raced Chihuahuas between the tufts. Gracie called an eye specialist, just in case. As soon as he gives the all clear we'll be out of here. We'll probably be home before you are.'

I sat stunned. This, I thought, must be what a moment of enlightenment is like, when suddenly everything is bright and OK. 'Appreciate your life,' Maezumi-roshi in Los Angeles said. I appreciated beyond words.

'Darcy?'

'Yes?'

'If you do get home first, take Duffy out.'

'Right. Love you, Mom.' My words surprised me. We Lotts don't gush. It didn't matter though; Mom had hung up.

Janice tucked away in safety, I pulled back onto the freeway and drove.

I hadn't realized how thick the air was. Mist here, but that's close enough to fog to make me feel at home. I could have wrapped it around my shoulders like the warm blanket I just hoped Janice was snuggled into.

After Mike disappeared I couldn't bear to stay in the city. I went away to college, as if I could learn a new identity there. I stayed on the east coast even though LA was the hub for stunt doubles. By the time I came back home, I'd been gone from the city almost as long as Mike had. I'd thought I was fine in the other fine places I'd lived and liked living in. I'd been fooling myself. Now, as the mist turned to fog, utter love of San Francisco engulfed me. I could have sung: *San Francisco, open your golden gate, da da da-da da-da.*

Suddenly I was exhausted. I fiddled around on the dashboard, hoping Gary had Janice Joplin at her loudest. John Philip Sousa, or Shostakovich. Whatever he had I couldn't find it. I opened the window and let the cold hit my skin.

Then I considered the question I hadn't had time to deal with. The body the sheriffs carried up from the cliff and shoved, dead, into the back of the van, the man they'd dragged from the water, was Grouch Marcus.

Grouch Marcus!

How had Grouch Marcus gotten himself killed?

Why had he wanted to ride up there with me?

He'd had Maria's cell number. He'd kept in touch with her all these years. Watched over the old burrito shop. Watched for what? Or who?

When I pulled off the road up north and Maria arrived, I'd left Grouch safe and warm in the car. Why had he left my car at all? He must have followed Maria and me. Had he stumbled over the cliff? Or did she push him over?

If he'd stumbled she would have gotten help.

So, why had Maria pushed Grouch Marcus over the cliff?

*Oh, Maria, no one thought of you, did they? You, the sweet girl ladling on the salsa? But here you are, alive, the owner of property, and living safe who knows where?*

# THIRTY

'You have assigned seats for breakfast?'

Despite being up all night, we all managed to laugh at Heather's question. The aroma of coffee, garlic and onions, mixed with eggs and homemade biscuits, had given us a second wind. Every one of us had a job that required all-nighters. Even Mom was ready to pop up at 3 a.m. to heat up some stew, or just listen while one of us sipped some *Powers* and grumbled or worried. The only eyes at half-mast were Boots's.

'Assigned seats? Not mandatory. Parking in the wrong chair doesn't get you ticketed . . .' Gary favored Heather with the subtly flirtatious smile with which he greeted new juries. It had to be second nature by now, which explained, in small part, his success in court and his three wives.

'Not ticketed, but I was eight before I realized other families said, "Good morning," not, "Get out of my seat."' Gracie reached for the coffee pot that sat in pride of place in the middle of the table. She hefted it, hesitated and poured. The rule was: he who empties has to refill, and no one wanted to leave their spot at the table just as Mom was hoisting the platter of eggs.

'You all ate breakfast together every morning?' Heather asked, as if she was on a zoo tour.

'Just Sundays,' I said.

'Before church?'

'Before football. Rule was – and this was a rule – that breakfast had to be over by 9.30 so Dad had time to digest before the 49ers gave him indigestion.'

'But didn't you—'

'Heather!'

I'd almost forgotten Boots was there.

'Excuse her. Her parents died when she was young, so she's always curious about real families. Mine too, but I moved in with my aunt next door, so it was like I just put my computer in a different bedroom. My mom's sister, so same rules, you know?'

Mom set the platter down in the middle of the table, and scooped out a portion for Boots. He waited. She scooped another. Again he waited. With a third, smaller spoonful, she smiled and said, 'It's going to be hard for you with these bandages,' and passed the platter to Heather. I could see each of my siblings recalculating their portions.

'All the time I was away I think this is the thing I missed the most, these breakfasts,' I said as the spoons were passed to the right.

'When Mike was gone?' Heather asked. 'That must have been so hard.'

Spoons clanked against the platter. And on Gracie's plate. Gary hit his coffee mug on the table as if by accident and Mom seemed to be stirring the refill eggs with undue ferocity. A more incisive observer than Heather – and apparently that would have been just about anyone – would have deduced that however we dealt with Mike's long absence, it wasn't verbally. We definitely – none of us – whined about our own hurt feelings. That person might have concluded that Mike not being at this meal was not a good sign. That person wouldn't be aware that the messages I had left him had gone unanswered, and that none of us knew where he was. That every one of us was worried. And we were not talking about that either.

Our relations with Mike had changed forever, but it was too soon to consider that. We'd have time – the rest of our lives, maybe – to wonder who he really was. What signs should we have noticed? Which ones did we see and push away?

Now we all looked at John. (Maybe we *were* regimented.) We had issues to discuss, plans to make. We were waiting for John to take charge. 'So here's what we know.' He forked up his last bite of egg. Already we knew he had OKed talking in front of Heather and Boots. 'Darcy?'

What I wanted to talk about was the body dragged up from the beach. But I knew I'd be interrupted ten times before I could get to my questions. So, the beginning . . . 'Mike said something was threatening him. A car hit him outside Gary's a couple weeks ago. Hit and run. Knocked him to the sidewalk—'

'Omigod!' Heather said. 'Was he hurt?'

Gracie shot her the stare of scorn. I'd seen her use it for other medical misassumptions.

'He said not. Make of that what you will,' I went on.

'What time was that, the hit-and-run?'

'Late, John. That's all he said. Columbus was pretty empty. He said he hadn't had to bother looking for traffic when he crossed the street.'

'It gets like that,' Gary muttered to his plate.

'That was a Tuesday,' I said. 'Friday morning he went out for a run—'

'That's his deal now,' Gary said. 'Says I suck the hours out his days. If he doesn't get to exercise in the morning, doesn't happen. Says, if he starts to leave the office, I figure he's got time to do some more filing.'

'He's right.' I'd temped for Gary. 'Anyway, he was sideswiped again. Cutting across the Embarcadero.'

'Jaywalking while people are trying to get to work. No one stopped, right?'

John was stating a fact more than answering a question, and I just nodded. 'Of course he said he wasn't hurt, not much anyway. But he took it seriously enough to find himself a temporary apartment.'

'The place beneath us?' Boots said between bites of scrambled eggs.

'Right. Just till Adrienne came back.'

'So, he sublet from this Adrienne?'

'She says not.'

Boots held up a bandaged hand, stopping Heather mid-fork. 'From Wally? Like us?'

Gracie had lost the coffee lottery contest and gotten up to make more. Mom had water boiling, so Gracie's penance was only pouring water into the pot and carting it back to the table. I reached for it.

'Wait, Darce. Give it time to clear the filter!'

'OK, OK! Here's my guess. I never got to ask Mike about it, but here's what I think. Janice said everyone knew Wally. *She* did. So chances were Mike did. So, he probably called him, assuming he'd know who could put him up for a few days. Long enough to figure out who was after him.'

'So, who was after him?' Boots said. 'I mean, there was the gas leak. That was aimed at him, right? And now this! What does he think?' He looked down at his bandaged hand, spotted with egg. 'Same guy as shot Wally?'

'Investigation's ongoing,' John said.

'Can't they run a make on the gun?'

'If it was registered in the city, yeah. In the state, maybe. It . . . No.'

'Adrienne said it wasn't hers. Mike told me it wasn't his.'

John just looked disgusted. But it was Gracie who said, 'Sure. Pack eight hundred fifty thousand people into a forty-seven-mile-square city. Toss in guns. What could go wrong? It's an epidemic.'

John, Gary and I started to speak at once. We'd all heard Gracie's rant before. It was Gary who prevailed. 'What we've got is an unknown perpetrator with an unclear object. Is he after Mike? All of us? Or whoever was in—' he glanced at Boots and Heather – 'or above Mike's temporary apartment. Whoever drove his car?'

'Oh, Darcy, that means you, doesn't it?' Mom was squeezing my shoulder.

I put my hand over hers. 'Probably. But I'm here shoveling down eggs. So, tough for the villain.' I plunked a forkful into my mouth. 'Mike followed me for two days trying to spot the guy, and to protect me. But nada. And then Wally was shot upstairs.' I eyed Boots and Heather. 'What do you guys know about that?'

What they knew boiled down to how inconvenient it is to have a murder in your temporary dwelling. 'I couldn't get my presentation notes! Or clothes,' Boots added. 'My suitcases were suddenly all "crime scene."'

'Mine?' Heather said. 'For all I know they're in San Francisco or in Spain or South America. I don't think I'm ever going to see them again. But that's minor compared to what you all are going through. Mike being gone all that time and now he could be killed.'

We definitely did not want to deal with that. 'Wally,' I said, 'info I got is he once knew everything going on, politically, socially. Wrote columns for counterculture papers occasionally. But word is his ship had sailed.'

'Maybe his sources drowned.' That from Gary. 'Or died of old age.'

'I'll tell you, I'd never have put money on him making it this long. All those years . . . If he didn't know, he didn't let on. If he did, he'd've choked before he'd do anything—'

'Doing nothing is doing something.'

We all stared at Heather for a moment.

'True,' John said, 'he could have cleared a lot of cases just by opening his mouth, prevented some aftermath. When the mayor was caught up with the trafficking, the circuit of teenaged girls from Vegas, etc., Wally knew all about it before we did. If he'd even hinted to us, we could have set up a sting and got to some of those girls before the circuit moved them on. If we could've pulled him in on some charge and held him we would have. He was a sly one.'

'Wow.'

We all stared at Boots.

'So he really did know people, way back? I figured he'd just had too much substance, you know?'

'So, you're saying Wally told you secrets from past city scandals and people who—'

'He would have, I think. But you know, we're paying a bundle to sleep in his place in order to talk about our ideas, our apps, our plans. If we want to listen to some old guy natter, we can do that at home.'

'Besides,' Heather said, 'Wally just knew local stuff. Names from twenty years ago in San Francisco don't mean anything to us.'

Gracie hefted the coffee pot, gauged the level of fullness and poured herself half a cup. 'Keeps coming back to: if someone was out to shoot him, they'd have done it ten or twenty years ago, not now.'

'Darcy?' Mom was standing behind me. Had she been there all along? 'Just what was it you were doing all night up there north of Santa Rosa?'

'Looking for Maria Perez. I had a lead to her from Jansen's Burritos, the place Mike and I . . . Maybe this is just too personal, you know. You don't mind, Boots? Heather?'

In the flurry of their dismissal I finished my eggs, reached for the coffee pot and reconsidered. Then I told my brothers and sister and mother that Mike had been transporting criminals from the coast to the city, beginning with Santino right before Mike disappeared.

'And after?' Gracie said.

'Santino killed four people. We had half the force looking for him!' John.

'Mike did that while he was "missing"?' Gary.

'He brought Santino into the city and let him go undercover? And kill people? Do you know the havoc?'

It seemed like there was a silence before Mom spoke. She said, 'All the time we thought he might be dead. He was driving into the city.'

She didn't say: He never called? He didn't care enough to let us know he was alive. Mom, who never left the house overnight all those years lest Mike came back and found it empty.

My gaze went blank. No one spoke. The silence seemed too thick to allow movement. I suspect the rest of them were having their own variations of my realization: the brother I thought was so special had faded away. Maybe he'd existed only in my imagination. Maybe he'd changed. But the man I had argued with on the pier a few days ago, later in Golden Gate Park resembled 'my' Mike, but he was a different being wearing that body.

I couldn't bring myself to believe that before. I did now.

I sat there, feeling like a cold cave had been carved into my gut.

Then I proved I was a Lott. I poured the rest of the coffee into my cup, swallowed some of it, and my feelings, and then told them about the safe house in Berkeley, Adrienne using it, Maria owning it. 'Thank Janice. When it comes to finding something or someone on the computer, she is the best. She discovered the Berkeley safe house's owner was near Point Arena. Grouch Marcus knew how to contact Maria. I—' I swallowed – 'drove him up there to meet Maria. Maria called Santino and I took her to rendezvous with him. She had a truck parked out of the way there; when she drove off I went after her. I lost her. I followed the sheriff back to near the original place Marcus and I met her. That's where I watched them bring up the body. It was Marcus.'

'No,' John said. 'You're wrong about that.'

'Excuse me?'

'I got an update from the sheriff. The man they pulled out of the water wasn't Marcus at all.'

'Listen, I saw—'

He held up his palm.

'Grouch Marcus, as you called him, never existed at all. The man they pulled from the water was Santino.'

# THIRTY-ONE

*Grouch Marcus, as you called him, never existed at all. The man they pulled from the water was Santino.*

I wanted to protest: *No, John, the body wasn't Santino. I saw him on the stretcher. It was Marcus. I drove the man up there, three hours in a car together.*

But John was saying, '"Marcus" looked like Santino because he *was* Santino. Santino, in the guise of Marcus.'

'What? That's not . . . How could . . .?'

Voices battered at me from all directions. 'How could that be?' is red meat to a Lott. They all had opinions, even Mom.

'How could it be?' I all but shouted. 'Marcus recognized me from when I was a kid at the taco stand.'

'He *said* he recognized you. Easy for him to say; no reason for you not to believe.'

Point for Gracie, there.

'What do you remember of his house?'

'Ramshackle. Sometimes Mike and I and the Perez girls sat on the steps. But we had to be careful for splinters. Splinters in the butt was a big joke then.'

'No one chased you?'

'No.' I thought about it a moment. 'Oh.'

'So, Darce, as far as you can say with confidence, you did not see any evidence of a man living in that house until today?'

'I was a kid. I got to scoop on the burrito line. Mike and I were on our way to the ball game.'

'*You* were headed to the ball game. Mike was setting up business.' Gary's voice was cold, steely, like a knife out of the fridge.

'*You* were cover.' John.

I pulled Duffy up onto my lap and stroked his chest. 'Be that as it may . . . OK, let's say Mike did pick up Santino at the coast and drive him to Jansen's. That's right before the earthquake. Then Mike disappeared.'

'Wise move. For him,' Gary muttered.

'Wise for all of us. No, listen, I'm not just going to bat for him. Suppose he'd stayed. Santino would have used us as leverage on him. He could have come after us one at a time. Like now.'

'Are you saying Mom was better off worrying every day that Mike was dead or—'

'I'm saying either way, same difference. She worried about him wherever he was. If he'd stayed here she would have worried about the danger to him here, or to you, Gracie, or any of us. And she'd have been right; he would have been in danger. I'm saying Mike chose the lesser of evils,' I said surprising myself. Outraged as I was, I hadn't intended to defend him. I could feel myself shaking.

'Probably one of a flock of safe houses, that shack,' John's elbows were braced on the table, as if the food had disappeared and he was back in the station house. 'That basement in Berkeley, bet we'll find Santino's fingerprints there. Place up near Point Arena. Who knows where else? Here's the beauty of it, no one's looking at those shacks; no one wants them in their line of sight. So there's no one wondering why they hadn't seen the old guy for a while. Santino can just pop in when he needs to.'

I was remembering what Maria said to me. 'The date of the shoot-out, when Santino shot those four people in the Mission, what was it?'

Phones leapt into hands.

I didn't wait for their confirmations. 'The first Thursday in April, right? The day Wally Ellis was shot.'

'Coincidence?' Gracie asked after a moment.

John snorted. 'I'll tell Higgins you spotted that.' A few moments passed in silence. He said, 'PD'll check it out.'

'But what's the connection?'

'PD'll find out; that's what we do. Let it go, Gracie.'

Mom reached for the empty egg platter. Spoons clattered. 'So,' she said, 'are you saying we're home free? Or just that we've done all we can?'

John just shrugged.

Gracie drew in a breath preparatory to combat, then suddenly gave it up, sighed and said, 'I've got a meeting in an hour. There's been an outbreak of Hanta Virus east of San Diego and . . . We done here?'

Gary finished his coffee in one swallow and stood. Duffy jumped off my lap.

'Hey, what about Wally? The man was murdered.'

'Wally,' John said, shaking his head. 'That's going to be one long case. Half the city had it in for him one time or another.'

'But not now,' I insisted.

'Darce, leave it to DD.'

*Not our problem.* But I didn't say that. We were a family that was full up on tension. No one wanted to sip from a stranger's glass.

Heather stuck her head in through the doorway; the idea of enduring more discomfort with her sad-sacking about it underlined the communal feeling.

And the scrum of pre-departure necessities began. Gary slid a ring of keys into my hand. He had to run, he insisted, but he was leaving me one of his other cars. Implicit in that was that I could cart the techies back downtown to wherever they'd be staying from here on in.

Suddenly Mom and I were alone in the kitchen. I grabbed the cups by the handles, slipped an arm in front of Mom at the sink and eased one batch in and then the other. 'You ought to get a dishwasher.'

She gave a thin laugh. 'I am the dishwasher.'

'What I mean—'

'I know. What you mean, Darcy, is that when Mike was gone, he was safe. When we brought him back, we robbed him of that.'

I nodded.

'We traded worry for danger. But here's the thing, honey: we traded fantasy for reality. That's what Leo would tell you, right?'

It was.

'Do you have a phone number for Mike?'

'A cell. If he checks it.'

'Give it to me.'

Mom herded the two techies back into the kitchen while I went upstairs to see if Janice had woken up. She was in her old room, one with dormer window that she liked. The room, though, always looked as if heat would skid to a stop at its door. The dormer faced the Pacific – 'my ocean view', she said with an irony that

Gary, Gracie and John never bothered to get. Her view, of course, was fog. It varied from heavy morning fog to the kind of dusting in the afternoon that allowed her to squint into the horizon and try to discriminate the gray blue above from the muddy blue below, and do it quick before serious fog rolled back in.

I sat on the edge of her bed. 'Glad you're not dead.'

'I'm not?' She glanced at the gray window.

'This is the last time I ever give you car keys, you know that, right?'

'That supposed to assure me I'm not dead?'

'Listen, I don't have much time. So, tell me what you found out about Wally Ellis. Was he in it with Santino? Two old guys about the same age.'

'Help me sit up.'

'Are you sure you—'

'Darcy, I have something you want.'

I smiled and helped, relieved at how much better than expected my sister seemed.

'There's a lot of data on Santino. It took me two hours to wade. You know one report says the same as another, as the one before that and before that, and then suddenly one has a line that's nowhere else. So you have to read every paragraph of every one.' She scrunched her shoulder and bent a knee preparatory to pushing herself up, and gasped.

I grabbed the sheet and held it away from her knee.

Janice, the nice one, never complained.

I said, 'And you discovered?'

'No connection between Wally and Santino. No hint, no speculation. And here's the take-away. There wasn't any connection, because Santino was shrewd and very, very careful. If he had had any need of Wally, he would have back-grounded him first and Santino would have concluded that a guy like Wally could never be trusted.'

'But Wally was known to never reveal—'

'Everyone's got their breaking point.'

'You sound like the Mafia.'

'Oh, little sister, you don't know the paths my fingers have taken.'

I didn't know whether to laugh or shiver. I said, 'But Wally must have heard that Santino was in the city. I mean, if Wally knew everything then—'

'Oh yeah, he knew.'

I raised an eyebrow and waited.

'Read Wally's column the day after Santino got to the city. The day before the shootings. If you read it contemporaneously it wouldn't mean anything to you. Wally covered himself that way. But read it a week later and Bingo!'

Janice's shoulders tightened. She was trying hard to keep herself upright, to keep me from seeing how hard she was trying.

'So, why was Wally shot?' Before she had to speak, I said, 'Mike aided Santino big time. He's been targeted big time. And yet, Mike's not dead. He was as easy a target as Wally, but he's not dead.'

She sagged down. I knew I should leave. She would answer my questions till the fog turned dark. She'd never complain, just go at it, query after positing, the way she had checking out Santino and Wally. The way she'd taken public transit into the city rather than inconveniencing me—

'Janice, how long did it take you to get to Mike's?'

'It wasn't bad.'

I didn't have time to break through her wall of non-suffering. 'No, listen, what time did you get to Mike's car?'

'Oh. I had to wait for BART – there was a hang-up on the Fremont line. So, it took me awhile to get in here on the train, get the streetcar. That was an hour and forty-five minutes. Then I walked a few blocks and—'

'What time . . .?'

'. . . Did the car blow up? 5.27.' She smiled weakly. 'So, yeah, that was after you drove Santino out of the city.'

I nodded.

She inhaled so hard the cords on her neck stood out. 'The explosive was triggered. Not on a timer. Set off when I got in.'

'Omigod.' I reached down to hug her, but she put up a hand. And I realized I didn't know where all her burns were. Instead I repeated, 'I'm glad you're not dead.'

It was a moment before I said, 'If someone set it off when you got in, they saw you get in. Me they might have mistaken for Mike, but not you.'

'I guess I was good enough.'
'Darcy!' Mom through the door.
'I'm leaving!'
I kissed Janice. 'I know I owe you.'
She just laughed. It seemed like all the effort she could make.
Mom was waiting in the hall. I said, 'It's not over.'
She nodded.
'Janice probably isn't the target. But you . . . Be careful, Mom.'

# THIRTY-TWO

The first surprise was the sun. We don't see it this early out here by the ocean. By the time I got downtown it would be warm and clear.

The second was car. Gary hadn't said a word about me driving the Aston through the mud and dirt. I had chosen to assume he was giving me a pass.

Until I saw the junker.

'My brother keeps an old car to loan to clients, or unreliable sisters.' Heather managed to creak open the passenger door but Boots had to brace a foot against the fender to get into the back. The stuffing was erupting from the seats. I cranked down the window an inch and it fell all the way. 'Thank god we don't need lights.'

'Hey Heather, you could come up with an app for that.'

'Huh?'

'For dealing with a car that's falling apart,' Boots explained.

'If you're driving this, you don't know what an app is.' *End of topic!*

I glanced over. She was staring ahead, blankly. She looked exhausted, though she must have had the best sleep of any night since she'd hauled herself up the stairs to Wally's apartment. Either our small talk was more than she could process, or she was too wiped out to bother.

Still, I asked, 'Did you ever get your luggage?'

'Huh?'

*Of course not.*

'Nah.' Boots was leaning forward over the back of the bench seat watching me wiggle the gear stick into reverse. 'I bought her the T-shirt so she'd have something clean to wear.'

'Where are you staying now, Heather?'

'Airport,' she said.

'I wanted to get her a hotel room, but she's all "No Way!" So we're camping out at SFO. My flight's at six in the morning, so no biggie.'

'And yours, Heather?'

'I'll just have time to wave him off and run.'

'Don't you need to get the burns on your hands checked again, Boots?'

'We've got doctors in Jersey.' He sounded desperate to be out of here.

I ended up driving them to SFO. And one look at Heather as she pushed out of the car in a short-sleeved yellow T-shirt with a dragon belching flags, just about had me pulling off my orange Polartec jacket and thrusting it at her. But she wouldn't need it; it was almost 70 degrees here.

And then it ended – not suddenly, like it had begun on the pier, but like a morning when the land fog is so thick it curtains off the sky and you keep turning over and going back to sleep. When you finally push yourself up, you discover it's been daylight for hours and you haven't realized it.

Mom had called Mike and said whatever words were her secret language with him. Mom never talked about one of her children with the others, and we, protective of our special relationships with her, did not discuss private talk lest we discover ours to be no more special than a sister's or brother's. We are an oddly wary bunch. But whatever she said, she was in charge of Mike now. I suspected he was home safe with her, no more leaving the house on his own than Duffy. For the moment.

Saturday, I threw myself into supporting the morning schedule at the Zen Center. We are still a small group, which means that jobs rotate fast among us. We aim to focus on the tasks before us. Cooking is the most essential for a schedule that runs from six in the morning till noon. Focus on chopping celery is the same as focus on your breath.

Be that as it may, people look forward to sitting the two periods of zazen as night gives way to the light of morning, to being an indistinguishable part of the sound of chanting, to the centuries-old choreography of the breakfast service.

I bowed as I entered the zendo. Shadows from the oil lamps shimmied along the walls. I bowed to my cushion on which I would gain enlightenment, and to the room, the community of us who would support each other's practice. And then the bell rang into silence.

After two periods of zazen, while the others were at the service, I made oatmeal, scooped out apple sauce and decanted the orange juice into pitchers. While they ate breakfast in the formal ritual in the zendo, I scrubbed the pots. Later I washed the breakfast dishes. I did the next thing. By noon I was back in bed.

By Tuesday I was edgy enough to call John and explain about my abrupt departure from the crime scene up north. I expected sparks, but he seemed fog-bound, too. 'Do you have anything to tell them that will move the case forward?'

'Nada!'

'Then save them the hassle.'

'I want to know if they traced the gun.'

'Save yourself the hassle. If they didn't pull up any record of it in twenty-four hours, it's not going to happen till no one remembers why they asked.'

'It's as if Wally Ellis wasn't just murdered but erased from existence.'

Gracie flung her cane out into the trash on the way to work Wednesday morning, and at eleven a.m. crashed into a desk and called me to race to her house before the garbage men arrived.

I picked up the phone to call Mike every day and put it down. I could have called Mom but I knew better.

Each passing day insisted more strongly that it was over. And yet the days felt like we were actors in front of a green screen.

Thursday the phone rang. My agent said, 'So, your video?'

'No hello? How are you?'

'I know how you are. Late.'

'Yeah,' I admitted. 'I'm sorry. Really. It would have been—'

'Skip it.'

*Sorry.*

'I got you an extension.'

I just stared at the phone. 'Every stuntwoman on the west coast will have sent a video. They must be overwhelmed. How could you get them to make an exception in order to get another one?'

'I'm good.' He gave the most minute of chuckles. 'I keep telling you – I'm that good.'

'I guess! What'd you tell *them*?'

'I said, "There's Darcy Lott and then there's everyone else. But don't take my word. Whittle your applicants down to five and then we'll send you Darcy's."'

I swallowed. 'You're not merely good, you are the best.'

'I know. But still, get it to me Monday.'

'You betcha!'

I have a file of cameramen. I could have called any of them. But I hesitated to say, 'How desperate are you for work? I'm offering you a couple-hour gig at rock-bottom rates. Odds are you won't get shot.'

Roman Westcoff had insisted he was a master at the end of a lens. Maybe. He'd take danger as a challenge. But the reporter might spot a lead, give chase and vanish halfway through the shoot.

So I called Mom. 'Let me talk to Mike.'

She didn't protest.

I didn't question that.

'Hi,' Mike sounded dead.

I said, 'This can't go on. I've got a plan. There are risks like—'

'I'm in.'

# THIRTY-THREE

We set up outside Renzo's at eight in the morning, Sunday, when the boutique architects' and law offices were closed, tourists weren't up, the strip clubs on Broadway a block away weren't within twelve hours of opening, and, with luck, only vehicle on Pacific Avenue would be a snazzy old blue Studebaker Renzo's cousin offered us.

'Here's the deal,' I said to Mike, and of course Renzo, who would have sold day-old muffins rather than miss a 'movie shoot' outside his cafe. The 'shoot' being merely an audition video didn't matter. Camera on café was camera on café. 'I walk out the door, turn to say goodbye, trip over something—'

'Not in my café! No one gets injured in here. No—'

'Sorry, Renzo! OK, so I walk out, turn to wave goodbye because I had such a wonderful experience, right? Then I trip over my own feet—'

Mike nodded. 'Funny,' said, barely looking at me. 'And easy.'

'Yeah. All skill. No props. Shows me off better.'

'Good shot of my new sign.'

When I'm planning a gag, I'm so deep in it, it's like I've slipped out of reality. Just the plan, the options, the problems, the alternatives. I heard Renzo's comments only enough to realize that in his mind the forty-five seconds would be a RENZO'S travelogue with me as a passing distraction. 'I catch myself before I hit the pavement, flail a bit—'

'Don't overdo,' Mike said.

'Not then. Then just a slightly exaggerated trip and catch. I right myself, step back and trip down the curb, catch—'

'More reaction.'

'Exactly. Trip, catch, and then just when it seems like I'm going to regain balance I fall back and splat onto the hood of a car.'

Mike was nodding as if he knew what I was talking about. I could have explained more but I hesitated to get into anything with him. He'd been waiting by Renzo's when I walked down the street just before 8.00 a.m. Even in the dullness of the gray morning, he shone like a deep red chrysanthemum on a lanky green stalk. A mum that was within days of being dead-headed. No sparkle in his blue eyes, no life apparent in his stance. He fingered his half-empty espresso cup, staring into it as if tea leaves had leapt in to warn him of danger.

Renzo prided himself on creating a new pastry every morning – the more exotic the mix, within the boundaries of tasty, the better. His lime and prosciutto turnover had scored a mention in the *Chronicle* food section. Today, though, he slid us a platter of plain, barely buttered buns that required concentration to bite and swallow. No saliva to be wasted on chat. I stared downward, chewed, and was grateful.

When my brother spoke his voice was so low I almost missed it. 'I never asked you to find me.' He swallowed. I couldn't tell if that motion was dealing with a lump of bun or emotion.

'I didn't ask you to put your life on hold, any of you.' He looked up, at me. 'It would have been better if you'd forgotten me back then, after the earthquake.'

'Easy for you to say—'

'No, dammit, not easy at all. I'm not good at this, being straight. If I was . . . But that's the thing. I'm not . . . I know what I am, Darcy. You've never known.'

I wasn't chewing, barely breathing.

'When I was a teenager it was fun to have a secret persona. But I boxed myself in with it. I only knew how to pretend—'

At the counter, dishes rattled in Renzo's hands.

Mike lowered his voice. 'What you want, Darce, doesn't exist. You, Mom, the rest of them. I can't—'

'Can't or won't?'

'Same thing.'

'So you're saying we're smothering you?'

'I nearly got you killed! You, Janice, Gracie; maybe Gary; maybe Mom. I didn't . . . I don't know what I didn't do. That's the thing. I've survived by keeping alert and when things get bad, splitting.'

'But—'

'It's not that I don't love you all. You and me, we were like . . .'

he pressed his forefinger and second finger together. The second was almost a knuckle longer. They looked like us walking side by side, him a head taller. 'It's like I've gone feral.'

'So, what? Should we put your bowl on the porch and hope if you come inside you don't pee on the carpet?'

He did a double-take, nodded, and said, 'Well, yeah I guess.'

'So, there's nothing you can do? You know, Mike, doing nothing is doing something.'

*Doing nothing is doing something.*

'I never asked you to find—'

'Fuck you!' I picked up my cup and drained it. We'd talk later. Maybe. Now I said, 'Is the action too much for forty-five seconds? There's a lot and I need time for my reactions. That's the important part.'

'I'll edit it down.'

*Fat chance!*

'Trust me.'

I didn't respond and those two words hung between us and then sank before I said, 'I'm trusting your camera work. A commercial like this could be huge for my career, not to mention wallet.'

'I'm good. Tr . . . Believe me.'

I did, on that. Mike was a fast learner and curious. He'd watched me set up a slip-and-fall sequence a month earlier, and by the next day he could do it himself. In the twenty years he'd lived in the shadows, I wondered how many things he'd mastered.

An overcast morning is pretty much the worst time to be setting up angles for a shoot that might begin hours later when the fog would have rolled back over the sea, and sun and shadows would stripe the shots. We had to hurry. If we didn't get the video in the can till noon or 1:00 p.m., the whole thing would be contrast, which would mean a different set of filters, maybe lenses. The gray sameness of the street and the shops across it would blare colors. Offices would cease to be backdrop. And Renzo's Caffe would so sparkle with old city charm that I would be no more than a bug flittering past. There was a lot to get down and I was glad of that. Mike might have thought I didn't know him, but I could tell he was glad, too.

I started blocking my moves, shot by shot – picturing stepping out of the cafe, the wave, my shoulders remaining part of the arm movement, my hips shifting into the turn as I started to walk to the street.

My foot hit the leg of a chair at a sidewalk table Renzo would bring later.

I stopped there, reran the sequence. Blocked each of my moves in my mind. Then ran it through in rehearsal mode.

'Angle's wrong.' Mike shifted position, forcing me to do the same. 'I don't want to chance getting street traffic in the background.'

As if to underline Mike's point, a silver van eased down the street. Minnesota plates. The driver slowed but didn't stop.

Across the street the sun was slicing shadows in the alleys between buildings. A man unlocked the gate to an antique shop. I saw a dark-haired woman so like Maria Perez I did a double-take, looked right and left. When I looked back she was gone. It made me wary. Why would Maria be in San Francisco? But, of course, she could have been here all along. San Francisco is a city of neighborhoods; she could have lived in the Mission or Noe Valley and never crossed paths with someone from the Sunset. She could have said she was a student at San Francisco State. People take classes there for years. No one would have questioned that. Like Mike had said about disguise, that people see what they expect to see and fill in around it. After she killed Santino, she might have gone anywhere.

We blocked the second sequence – the recovery from the trip and almost-fall on to the misstep off the curb – then the stumble, the recovery, and the stagger back on to the car hood. If I'd been setting up for a movie, that could involve a dozen takes. I would have padded the curb, painted the padding to match, the way it's done in a stair fall. I would definitely have run a strip of padding along the hood of the Studebaker. But finding a color to match it – well, that's why second unit directors have assistants. I'd have given special attention to any spot my hand would land on. A sprained or broken wrist can haunt you for years. As it was, the whole set-up took nearly three hours, and the run-through of it all together, another.

Mike went to pick up pizza. I changed into an orange leotard, applied the kind of make-up stunt doubles never need. I made a couple calls. The sun was bright now. Renzo's sign sparkled like it was the entrance to heaven. When Mike got back, we ate pizza, adjusted shot plans, focused like a brace of dogs carrying a single huge bone in their mouths.

I did trust him. I trusted him to scan the street, the dark exits of alleyways between buildings, the trees that were not quite wide enough to hide a person. He'd be shooting east on Pacific, in order to get the Studebaker as it approached slowly – we'd speed it up in 'post-production' – along this one-way street. But I knew every time his eyes left the camera's eyepiece he'd be checking the traffic on Columbus as it flowed toward downtown, the freeway, the bridge.

What I did not trust him to do was to pay enough attention to get decent shots of me. For that, I had three back-ups, one in the attic/air space above Renzo's with a good line of sight, one in an alleyway across the street, back far enough so the light didn't reflect off his lens. Back so far it – alas – limited his shots. And Renzo had had a video cam mounted on the Studebaker's dashboard.

I did not tell Mike any of that.

I watched my brother walk toward the camera, his gait long and easy, one I would recognize in any sized crowd, his hair the same dark red as mine, only a bit curlier. This stranger in that familiar body.

All the years I had missed him, longed to find him, I'd dreamed of having him back in the family, the way we were. Now even the dream was gone. I felt lonelier than I ever had.

I walked up to him, moving him back from the camera and hugged him long and hard.

I wasn't surprised that the gunshot came then. Later Heather would say she'd intended to wait for the perfect moment, but seeing Mike there, the man who had driven her parents' killer to San Francisco . . . seeing him embraced by his family, a family like the one that had been ripped away from her, she couldn't keep herself from shooting.

She was a good shot. The first bullet nicked my upper arm and ripped through Mike's ribs. If he hadn't been so much taller than me, he'd have been dead. I shoved him down. Bullets hit his jacket, his hair. The last one cracked his humerus. All before the auxiliary cameramen a.k.a. police photographers grabbed her. Even then she managed to throw the Glock hard into Mike's back.

I wanted to ask her, 'Was that enough?' But her face slowly took on the empty look of a dead dream. I could have said, 'Once this hits the papers, your parents' death won't be collateral damage any more,' but I wasn't going to give her that either. Instead I asked about Wally.

After they cuffed her, I said, 'Wally? You lived with him. You liked him, kind of, didn't you?'

'Yeah.'

I thought she'd go on. When she didn't, I said for her, 'But he knew Santino shot your parents. And he did nothing.'

*Sometimes doing nothing is doing something.*